D0492130

DAY OF THE GUN

The county of Singletree, Montana has a problem with rustlers. Cyrus McCall strings barbed wire between his land and that of his neighbour, Maggie Carter. But this means that Maggie must herd her cows an extra two miles to their drinking water, taking time and manpower she can't spare — not to mention implying she is in league with the rustlers who push stolen stock across her land. Maggie promises hell if the fences aren't taken down — and hell is what she and McCall will get . . .

BEN BRIDGES

---◆---

DAY
OF THE
GUN

Complete and Unabridged

LINFORD
Leicester

First published in Great Britain in 2014

First Linford Edition
published 2015

Based upon the screenplay by Wayne Shipley

Names, characters and incidents in this book are
fictional, and any resemblance to actual events,
locales, organizations, or persons living or dead is
purely coincidental

A catalogue record for this book is available
from the British Library.

ISBN 978–1–4448–2498–8

Published by
F. A. Thorpe (Publishing)
Anstey, Leicestershire

Set by Words & Graphics Ltd.
Anstey, Leicestershire
Printed and bound in Great Britain by
T. J. International Ltd., Padstow, Cornwall

This book is printed on acid-free paper

Dedicated to the Cast and Crew of
Day of the Gun

1

In a land and time where it was nothing for a town to spring up, boom and then die in what seemed like the blink of an eye, Singletree, Montana had one distinct claim to fame: it was just about to commemorate its silver jubilee.

The town had gotten its name when a broken singletree — the swinging bar that connects an animal harness to a wagon — had forced prospector Hiram Polk to delay what had otherwise been a largely unremarkable journey west. A devout man, Polk had promptly taken the accident as a sign and staked his claim right where he was. Soon, other miners joined him, and before long Singletree — by this time a handful of tents and a cabin or two — was well on the way to becoming a boomtown.

The only difference was that this particular boomtown *flourished*.

Most of the gold, silver, copper and coal mines thereabouts proved profitable, businesses sprang up to cater for the sudden influx of pitmen and the entrepreneurs who employed them, and before long local ranchers also started coming in for supplies.

Within a year, Singletree could boast more than just three saloons and an assay office. The addition of a livery, a sprinkling of general stores, two boarding houses, a restaurant, church, school and even a local newspaper, the Singletree *Enterprise*, all helped turn it into a fully-fledged metropolis. When the Northern Pacific laid its tracks on the outskirts of town and established a stopover there back in '87, its status was sealed.

But Singletree had its problems, too.

The country thereabouts had recently been targeted by rustlers, and to make matters worse, there seemed to be no set pattern to their raids. Some dark nights the cattle-lifters made off with as little as ten head; others, they laid claim to as many as thirty. And they never left any clues behind them. There were never any trails to follow, no butchering sites to be discovered, no reports from the railhead — not even a stray hide with a recognizable brand. It was as if the stolen cattle simply . . . disappeared.

That being the case, there was little that the local Stock Growers Association could do about it. And as diligent as he was, County Sheriff Matthew McKenna was similarly helpless.

On the day that Singletree celebrated its twenty-fifth year, Cyrus McCall, owner of Big Sky Ranch, was mad enough to wake snakes. The night before, he'd lost another twenty-five head. The thieves had simply cut his wire and helped themselves.

Though fiercely loyal to the brand, however, McCall's hired hands were too excited about the coming festivities to worry overmuch about rustlers right then. They figured that Big Sky was large enough to withstand the losses, and McCall could indeed suffer them better than most. But it was the

3

principle of the thing that sat like a burr in the grizzled rancher's metaphorical boot. He was a man of action, and he hadn't built up the biggest spread in the region by avoiding action when action was needed.

But who, exactly, was he supposed to take action *against?*

Hoping to avoid their boss's wrath, the hands headed for town instead, there to eat, drink and socialize well out of McCall's sight. As far as they were concerned, nothing was going to stall or otherwise spoil their enjoyment of the elaborate plans the town had made to celebrate its jubilee. High among these was what the Jubilee Committee called 'The Baseball Game of the Decade,' which promised to pit a local pickup team against the notorious Excelsior Aces, a traveling team with a nearly perfect record and a reputation for no-holds-barred tactics.

No wonder, then, that the mood in Singletree that day was one of high excitement and great civic pride. Signs

4

and banners had been erected along Main Street to proclaim the town's unique place in the state. Red, white and blue bunting, strung from one false front to its equivalent on the opposite side of the street, flapped and fluttered in the gentle breeze. Beneath its skittering shadows old friends renewed acquaintance, swapped news and shared jokes, while Simon Doubleday, who owned and ran the *Enterprise*, did his best to be everywhere at once, gathering quotes and scribbling hurried observations in the certain knowledge that his next edition would be a sellout.

The women of the Church League had done the town proud, and gingham-covered trestle tables ran the length of Main. There were cherry pies and stuffed turkey, fried and mashed potatoes and hot rolls; squash, turnips and puddings made from apples and breadcrumbs. There was hot coffee and ice-cream sodas, root beer and a dozen huge bowls of Ada Curtis' secret-recipe sour-apple punch.

Children cried or laughed and ate too

much. The town's 'first citizen' — who just so happened to be an eight-year-old molly mule called Grace — was allowed to roam the streets at will. And up at the far end of town, the members of the Singletree Marching Band entertained passers-by with sometimes melodic, sometimes God-awful renditions of *In The Good Old Summertime*, *After the Ball* and *The Esquimaux Dance*.

As people began to wander down to the field where the baseball game would soon get underway, Maggie Carter rode into town alongside the Carter Ranch supply wagon, on the seat of which slouched Nelson Nubbins, a hulking, slope-shouldered man in his late fifties who was known to all simply as 'Nubbs.'

Maggie was a short, feisty woman of forty-five, with a shock of red-auburn hair spilling from beneath an old, unflattering gray hat with a center dent. Her garb was strictly practical: a high-necked Abbington blouse under a creased box jacket, and a full-cut riding skirt over boy's-size Justin boots. Like the woman herself, there was no time for frills or fancies here.

Now, as she surveyed all the merriment around her, her lips curled disparagingly. Since the death of her husband Charles two years earlier, Maggie has grown increasingly intolerant of celebrations of any kind. As much as anything else, she figured they were a waste of time — and time was something that always seemed to be in short supply where Maggie was concerned. She had a ranch to run — a tough enough job for a woman even at the best of times, but made more difficult still since Cyrus McCall had strung a barbed wire fence adjacent to her property in an attempt to foil the rustlers.

The only reason she was in town today — and hating the frivolity that met her at every turn — was to meet her twenty-one year-old daughter, Kate, who was returning home from St. Louis, where she'd been in school.

Indeed, Kate was another reason for

Maggie's disquiet. She hadn't seen her raven-haired daughter since the funeral, and was fully expecting Kate to have changed out of all recognition over the last two years. She would have matured — hopefully — and developed opinions of her own, for she had always favored her mother in that respect. But Maggie had a feeling that Kate would also find that she had outgrown Singletree — and quite probably the whole of Montana.

No matter how civilized Singletree now considered itself to be, it still couldn't hold a candle to the thriving metropolis of 1895 St. Louis. Maggie had a feeling that Kate would now take one fresh look at the town and its environs and wonder how she could ever have been satisfied to live here and not pine for the outside world.

In one way it would please her to see the girl show some ambition, to want more than she already had. But in another, Maggie knew that the future of the C.A. Carter Ranch lay in Kate's hands, for Kate's brother, Ned . . . well, much as it pained her to admit it, Maggie could find no faith in her that Ned would ever take over the running of the ranch.

And talking of Ned . . .

As Maggie and Nubbs plowed through the crowd heading for the game, Maggie spotted a familiar palomino gelding tied to the crowded hitch-rack outside Georgia Lamb's saloon. The sight did nothing to improve her temper. Recently, Ned had been spending more and more time away from home, and she had learned from questioning her foreman, Wade Palmer, that he'd entered into a relationship with the saloon's fiery owner.

Impulsively, and without a single word to Nubbs, Maggie now turned her horse toward the saloon, suddenly set on catching her son *in flagrante delicto*. Nubbs could only watch her go, knowing there was nothing he or anyone else could do to stop her. That woman had a mind of her own: always had. In any case, Nubbs had no need to go with her, for he reckoned Maggie was more than capable of dealing with whatever trouble she stirred up with Ned and Georgia.

Besides, Nubbs was set on being there when Kathryn Elizabeth Carter stepped down off that train. He'd always been devoted to her, and her long absence had served only to make him grow even fonder of her than he had been before.

He hauled rein outside the weathered plank depot and climbed down, his movements as slow and precise as ever. He looked disreputable in his well-worn oilskin duster and boots run down at the heels, and his gunmetal-gray hair hung long, limp and lackluster from beneath his stained Tucson hat. But for all that he was as dependable as pumpkin pie and stuffing.

He was what Charlie Carter had always called 'silent by choice.' He *could* speak, but hadn't uttered a word since being captured and hanged by Confederate troops during the Great War. Charlie Carter, under whom he had served as a sniper, had risked his own life to scatter the enemy and cut Nubbs down before he could strangle to death, and Nubbs, with his small, sad eyes and jowly, hangdog expression, had been fiercely loyal to the Carters ever since.

From beneath the wagon seat he now took a small package wrapped in sacking, and with this tucked beneath one arm, he climbed the steps to the platform. As he did so, he heard a shrill whistle in the distance, and a few moments later saw the big Baldwin locomotive round a distant bend in the track, belching smoke from its diamond stack.

As the train chuffed steadily closer, the engineer started clanging the bell. It should have brought folks running, for the arrival of the day's train was still a source of high excitement, even eight years on. But today folks had other things on their minds, and Nubbs more or less had the platform to himself.

He felt a sudden flutter of nerves. Up to now he'd always looked upon Kathryn as his little Kate. But Kate wasn't so little anymore. She was a woman now, and he doubted that she'd want a seedy old specimen like him to keep fussing around her.

Suddenly anxious, he touched the red neckerchief beneath which the scars of the noose still seemed so fresh to him.

Moments later the loco floated in on a cushion of billowing steam. Nubbs hastily polished the tops of his boots against the calves of his jeans, and then squared his shoulders. The loco shushed past him with a squeal of brakes, jolted to a shuddering halt . . . and a few moments later, there she was.

Kathryn.

She climbed down the iron steps at the far end of the first Pullman carrying two carpetbags, and even though the journey had been a long one she still somehow managed to look as fresh as a daisy. She saw Nubbs at the same moment he saw her, and when he saw the softening of her features and realized that she still looked upon him as a second father, he knew he'd been foolish ever to worry the way he had. Kathryn might have become a woman, but in every other respect — at least where he was concerned — she hadn't changed a bit.

She hurried toward him, tall and slim in a teal-colored outing jacket and matching skirt, her dark hair pinned high beneath a matching riding hat covered in lace. She dropped her bags at her feet and hugged him tight, and Nubbs, who never had quite figured out how to react to such open displays of affection, blushed furiously.

At last Kate stood back and studied him. Her clear skin was the color of alabaster, a little flushed now from the trapped heat of the railroad car. She had a button nose beneath which sat a Cupid's bow mouth and a firm, oval jaw, and as she looked at him, tears shone in eyes that he'd always likened to large blue sapphires.

For her part, she thought simply, *Nubbs*. He'd always been there for her, and she suspected he always would be, no matter where life took her. And she wouldn't have it any other way.

'Cat got your tongue, Nubbs?' she teased at last.

He shrugged awkwardly.

'You know, Mr. Nelson Nubbins,' she continued playfully, 'now that I'm an educated woman, I dub you the ideal male of the species — forever silent! What more could a woman ask for?'

Nubbs grinned shyly, then took the package from beneath his arm. From the sacking he withdrew a beautifully-carved box. He'd been working on it for the past two years, ever since Kate had left for St. Louis.

He handed it to her. She was speechless at the intricacy of it, the fact that it was in the truest sense a labor of love, and she had to look down at her feet for a long beat until she could compose herself again. 'Nubbs,' she managed after a while, 'I . . . ' She shook her head as words deserted her. 'It's *beautiful.*'

The sound of approaching hooves brought Nubbs around just as Maggie rode up. As usual, Maggie's expression was almost impossible to read. It told nothing of what had transpired at the saloon — indeed, if *anything* had transpired. In all probability, Nubbs thought, Ned had probably hidden beneath Georgia Lamb's blankets while Georgia told Maggie that her son wasn't there.

Now Maggie's green eyes moved to her daughter and evaluated her frankly. 'Your father would be proud of you,' she said at last.

Kate looked up at her, closing one eye against the brightness of the day. 'And my mother?' she asked guardedly.

Maggie hesitated, then said with the curious formality that had come to be her hallmark, 'Approval must be earned.'

Letting that last comment pass, Kate scanned the bustling street behind her. 'I'd hoped to see Big Brother on that little yellow mare of his.'

Nubbs winced. If he knew Maggie, any mention of Ned was strictly off-limits right then. Sure enough, Maggie's only response was a terse, 'I'd best be going. I'll see you later, at supper.'

And with those words she turned her horse and rode away, leaving Nubbs to pick up Kate's bags and accompany her to the wagon.

★　★　★

Appearances of the Excelsior Aces regularly drew crowds well into the hundreds. Most of the players were skilled enough for a career in the minor leagues, but rather than put up with rules, regulations and rigorous training schedules, they'd opted for the life of barnstormers because it gave them the chance to see different towns, saloons and women several times each month.

When they took to the field to warm up, townsfolk and visitors alike crowded the third-base line to get a closer look at them. Big, burly men, they nevertheless moved with power and grace. Their black and red uniforms set them apart from the local players, who wouldn't have had any way of identifying themselves were it not for the generous efforts of a local seamstress, who'd made them all blue caps.

The Aces' business manager, Pepper Dean, was friends with mine owner and Singletree mayor, Wesley Rickey. After some negotiation they'd agreed to stage today's event using the rules that were in place in the 1860s, when Singletree was founded. Among other things, that meant no gloves were allowed, no overhand pitching and, perhaps most importantly of all, a fly ball caught on one bounce was an out.

Just before the game commenced, Singletree took to the field to show off a bit itself. At their entrance, the

17

Singletree Marching Band struck up *The Washington Post March*.

The teams filed out onto the impromptu field and the band came to an untidy finish as the formalities were observed. For a moment there seemed to be some confusion among the officials. Then word began to spread — the organizers had thought of everything but who would call the game. After a while a reluctant Reverend Arthur Braxton — probably the only man both teams trusted — was pressed into service.

'*Striker to the plate!*' he yelled. '*Striker to the plate!*'

The game got off to an impressive start, and as the first few innings moved along, there was plenty of action for everyone. To the surprise of all, the hometown team — while still behind the Aces — put up a real fight, and it quickly became apparent that this was not going to be the rout the Aces had been expecting. So when the hotheaded team captain Joe 'Silver' King stepped up to the line to face Singletree pitcher Val McCall, son of rancher Cyrus, he had blood in his eye. He was going to show these hicks just what the Aces were made of, and if there were a few casualties along the way, then so be it.

Hugging the third-base line was first citizen Gracie. Somehow the molly mule seemed to sense the striker's intentions, and knew just what to do to rattle him.

Every time Joe swung the bat, Gracie brayed so loudly that it caused him to miss the throw. The fact that this brought jeers and laughter from the onlookers cut him like a rusty blade. After two more missed strikes, Joe got positively mad. When the next ball was thrown, he dropped the bat, caught the ball — then turned and let it fly right at Gracie.

The five-and-one-eighth-ounce ball struck the mule hard on the neck. With a high-pitched bray she sidestepped nervously.

For one shocked moment, the assembled townsfolk could hardly believe their eyes.

Even Pepper Dean cringed.

Silence settled over the field. Then one little girl, filled with indignation, broke away from her mother, trotted across the field and without hesitation kicked Joe in the shin.

Again there seemed to be a collective sigh of indrawn breath. For a moment afterward, it was within Joe's grasp to win back the crowd by taking it with good humor and ruffling the little girl's hair fondly. Had he shown even a *little* contrition, Singletree might have forgiven him his momentary lapse.

Instead, he put a big, callused palm over the little girl's face and shoved her to the ground, and as far as Val McCall was concerned, that was *it*.

Mouth clamped tight and square jaw thrust forward, Val quit the pitcher's line and went right after him, and in almost the same moment the rest of the Aces rushed forward to defend him. In next to no time the two opposing teams clashed in combat, and fists started flying left and right. In a desperate attempt to break up the fight, the Singletree Marching Band started playing *Onward Christian Soldiers*, but to no avail.

★ ★ ★

The fight was well underway when Nubbs angled the supply wagon around the edge of the field and onto the trace that would take it back to the ranch.

Now seated beside him, Kate watched the brawl with a disapproving shake of the head. She had no way of knowing, of course, that the local team was fighting to defend the honor of the little girl who'd been pushed over, or the molly mule at whom the ball had been thrown. To Kate it was clear; these were men, and what could be more fitting to a man's nature than that he fight on even the slightest pretext?

Then, without warning, one of the Singletree players suddenly staggered free of the mêlée, and straightening up, turned her way.

It was Val McCall, looking disheveled and sweaty, cap lost, blond hair awry.

They spotted each other in the same moment, and even from a twenty-yard distance each saw something in the other's expression that went beyond the mere recognition of a childhood friend long unseen. As Kate looked into his clean-shaven face, with its normally gentle hazel eyes and high cheekbones, she suddenly flustered, uncomfortable with her own feelings. Quickly, she looked away from him, leaving Val to watch her go, the fight temporarily forgotten . . . until one of the Aces tackled him from the side and took him down in a heap.

★　★　★

When the dust finally settled in the field just outside Singletree, Montana, a bruised ego was the most prevalent injury. And even though the Excelsior Aces had notched up more runs before all hell broke loose, everyone in town knew that on that day of Singletree's twenty-fifth birthday, the Singletree team had trumped their opponents when it came to fisticuffs . . . and had done so in style.

2

Considering they hadn't seen each other for two years, Maggie didn't exactly go out of her way to spend much time with Kate following her return home. To practical, no-nonsense Maggie, time was always to be used productively, and never frittered away on idle conversation. Besides, she had other things on her mind. Sometimes it seemed she *always* had other things on her mind.

Kate knew better than to take it personally. They'd never been especially close, and she could hardly see the situation changing now. Maggie — it had always been hard for Kate to think of her in terms of 'Mother' — had always been driven to succeed. The daughter of Irish immigrants, she'd grown up poor in Tennessee, and following the death of her husband,

Maggie's mother had been taken in by a violent drunk called Abraham Tanner, who'd bullied, beaten and finally broken her. They'd been dark days indeed, and they'd darkened still more when Maggie herself had come to Tanner's attention.

Although no one else knew it, her stepfather had finally seized his opportunity, overpowered her and raped her. But the next time he'd tried it she'd shot him with her father's old Navy Colt. She might even have shot him again and ended his wicked ways once and for all if it hadn't been for the intervention of her mother.

As it was, Abraham Tanner took the .36 ball in his upper left arm, and before he could recover enough to get his revenge, Maggie left home and somehow wound up as a laundress in Singletree. Of course, the town had been plenty raw back then, and no place for a shrinking violet. Maggie had been forced to toughen up even more in order to survive and make something of herself.

In fact, Kate had often speculated that it was Maggie's desire to succeed that first attracted her father. Though bright and resourceful, the late War had killed something in Charlie Carter, and he and Nubbs had moved west to the Montana Territory, as it then was, in the hope that they might yet find peace again.

The way her father told it, it was love at first sight when he'd encountered Maggie. 'There she was,' he used to say, 'scrubbin' the filth off a miner's clothes, with a great big soap bubble on the end of her nose — '

'No I did not!'

' — and you know somethin'?' Charlie Carter would continue, as if Maggie hadn't interrupted him, 'I fell in love with her right there and then.'

What he didn't say — what he didn't even *realize*, perhaps — was that Maggie had found something in his sincere and sober temperament that helped her overcome her by-now instinctive mistrust of men. They married within the month and the following spring Maggie gave birth to Kate's brother, Ned. Kate herself was born three years later.

Even then, however, theirs had never been a conventional 'family' life, exactly. Maggie was too domineering for that, too ambitious for her husband, her children and the ranch. More than once, Charlie would tell folks that the only reason the C.A. Carter Ranch grew so fast and enjoyed such success was because 'Maggie just wouldn't let a man quit.'

Then, right out of the blue, Charlie Carter caught pneumonia and died. And after that it was almost as if Maggie decided to turn the ranch into a monument to her late husband. Perhaps his passing reminded her that time was precious and that she had to make every second count. But in so doing, there grew between mother and daughter (and mother and son) a peculiar and sometimes hard-to-define distance — of something that could no longer truly be called a *relationship*.

Sometimes, Kate wondered if the most important thing to Maggie was the ranch. Perhaps it was — it was certainly something over which she was able to exercise control. She'd had little luck where Kate was concerned, and even less, Kate suspected, with Ned.

Early one morning a few days later, Kate led her father's favorite mottled gray horse, Whiskey, out of his stall and set to work on him with a currycomb. The horse was eighteen years old now, but in human terms he was in his fifties, and it had started to show. His long face had somehow hollowed out, especially around the eyes, and his lower lip drooped in a way it hadn't done just two years earlier. There were white hairs around his eyes, ears, forehead and muzzle, and the eyes themselves were no longer as sharp as they used to be.

'Rest his soul, Father doted on you somewhat more than was in your best interest,' she murmured as she worked on the animal. 'While the rest of the

28

remuda worked day in and day out, you were allowed to grow fat and lazy, trotted out only on Sundays and when he had to attend Stock Growers meetings. You're a looker, as Father used to say, but you've been neglected these past two years, haven't you?'

At that moment a shadow filled the barn doorway, darkening the interior a fraction, and when she looked around she saw Ned standing there, watching her. He came deeper into the barn and led his own palomino from its stall. It was a magnificent animal, and Whiskey didn't compare favorably.

'Going for a ride?' Kate asked by way of greeting.

Ned draped a blanket across his horse's back. 'Got any objections?' he countered.

Kate bit back a response. It had nearly always been hard work, engaging Ned in conversation. 'That yellow horse of yours is a looker,' she said. 'But does she earn her keep?'

He glanced at her, so pale in the

hay-smelling gloom that he looked almost ghostly, his skin the color of tallow. 'And then some,' he replied, adding, 'Miss-Kathryn-Carter-What-Business-Is-It-Of-Yours?'

'Just curious, Big Brother.'

She looked at him a moment longer. Beneath his workday range clothes he was of average height and slight build, his facial features soft and boyish and completely at odds with his hazel eyes, which somehow seemed to belong to an older, sadder man. Once handsome, his good looks were now marred by a deep, dark scar that stretched like an upside-down letter *Y* from his left eyebrow to his baby-smooth jaw line.

'Remember the day Father brought that little filly home for you?' she asked, hoping to lighten his ever-present dark mood. 'Mother wouldn't speak to him for a week when she found out he'd swapped two broke cow ponies for her.'

'I remember,' he said. His voice was little more than a weak, defeated sigh, as if all the fight had gone out of him.

'She never understood how just havin' something could make you feel.'

'You miss him, don't you, Ned? Father?'

'Know something, sis?' he asked. 'I'm used to it. Losing things . . . that's what life's all about. Leastways, mine is. Learned to live with it. Hell, learned to *expect* it, half the time.'

'It doesn't have to be that way, Ned.'

'Does for me,' he said tersely, and continued saddling up.

'I miss him most at the supper table,' Kate confessed, still thinking about their father. 'Remember how he used to make his Adam's apple jump when Mother wasn't looking, and how we'd laugh? Even Nubbs would crack a smile. Then he'd say, 'Margaret, I think you better teach these ragamuffins some manners.''

Ned's sudden grin stretched the scar a little. 'Yeah. 'Teach these ragamuffins some manners.' And then she'd give us the evil eye, and that only made us laugh even more.'

'Remember that time we just couldn't stop? Mother made us leave the table.'

He nodded. 'I don't know why we just didn't tell on him.'

'I do,' she replied. 'Because we loved it.'

All at once his good humor seemed to evaporate.

'Ned,' she began.

'What now?' he asked sourly.

'I just . . . wondered. Do you still see Molly Richfield? I mean, talk to her or anything?'

'Molly's gone,' he replied shortly. 'A riddance I no longer care to think on.'

'What happened?'

'What do you think happened? She ran off with a drummer, about eighteen months ago.'

'And Val?'

'What about him?'

'Did you two ever . . . patch things up again?'

His eyes grew flinty. 'He's dead to me,' he said.

'But you two were like brothers.'

'I said he's *dead* to me. And if you've got any sense, you'll stay away from him as well.'

He turned his back on her and briskly finished saddling the palomino. She watched him for a while, wanting to reach out to him somehow, to make him open up and let go of all the poison that had filled him up, but she knew better than to try. The more you tried with Ned, the less you were likely to succeed. But one day, she hoped, he would open up and talk to her of his own accord, and then he might finally start to heal.

At last he led his horse out into the new day, and without a parting word mounted up and rode out. Kate finished working on Whiskey, and led him out into the growing sunshine a short time later.

Maggie was on the far side of the yard, talking with Wade Palmer. Kate felt her mother's eyes on her almost immediately. She pretended not to notice, but secretly she hoped that her mother would see the care she, Kate, had lavished on the ageing mount. As he stood there now, Whiskey looked slicker than he had in years.

'Are you going for a ride?' Maggie called as she strode across the yard a moment later.

Kate nodded. 'I thought it was about time I saw the ranch up close again.'

'A brave choice for a mount,' said Maggie, gesturing to the horse. 'Whiskey hasn't carried weight since your father last sat him. He's apt to be full of himself.'

'I doubt that. Father never owned a mean horse in his life.'

'I didn't say he was *mean*,' Maggie corrected. 'Just that he's come to . . . value his leisure.'

'Well, he's got a woman in his life now, who's not about to let him go to seed.'

Maggie's lips narrowed, hearing that. 'You have a high opinion of yourself, don't you, Kathryn?'

'I don't mean to. All I'm saying is

that the male of the species simply needs a job, something to accomplish. We women provide the motivation, the . . . *direction.*'

'A horse is one thing,' Maggie said at length. 'But I don't see you providing much . . . *direction* . . . to anything on two legs.'

'You're talking about William Sinclair, I assume?'

'Well, what happened to him? When you first went to St. Louis, your letters were full of him. But you haven't said a word about him since you came back.'

'I . . . don't really know what to *say.*'

'He has taste, culture. He comes from a good family. He's easy on the eye — and he dotes on you.'

'He's all of that,' said Kate.

'But . . . ?'

'William doesn't *need* direction,' Kate replied at last. 'He already knows exactly where he's going. And though he does, as you say, profess boundless devotion and wants me to share his good fortune, I suspect I'm only there to sit at his right hand, mouth shut, smiling demurely.'

'Better that than tears, callused hands and a back bent with little to show for it.'

'You mean the ranch? That's the difference, mother. You and father built this place *together*, had an equal say in just about everything. All right, so it's got splinters and weeds, but it's *alive*. It came from you, from the *two* of you! You can breathe it and feel it, it courses through your veins and becomes a part of you. You can't avoid it — it won't let you. And when you look around . . . why would anyone *want* to avoid it?'

Although she was pleased to hear it, Maggie said harshly, 'It killed your father.'

'I can't agree with that. But even if it did, he wouldn't have walked away from it for anything — and you wouldn't have let him.'

Maggie shifted weight. 'Understand something, Kathryn,' she said. 'There's no romance in digging and clawing for everything you get. I *know*.'

'Who says I *want* romance?' Kate countered. 'All I want right now is the life I've got — and the right to live it as I see fit.'

Maggie gave a short, dismissive laugh, as if she found the idea amusing. 'If you *live* it, as you say, then you'll find that life has a way of running away from you. Your brother, for instance. Having to deal with him drains me. It drains me far more than it should.'

'Ned is Ned, Mother. It was hard on all of us when we lost Father, but Ned took it harder than anyone. You always wanted so much for him. How do you think he feels when he can't be what you want? He'll come around eventually, but you've got to give him a chance to — '

'When you've experienced motherhood yourself,' Maggie interrupted stiffly, 'then I might consider your advice.'

Kate drew a breath. 'Fair enough.'

37

And then, to change the subject, 'I thought it was about time Whiskey found his wind again.'

'Wind?' Maggie summoned a smile, happy to change the subject herself. 'That crowbait never could run more than a hundred yards without folding his tent.'

'Is that a fact?' asked Kate, raising one fine brow. And then, impulsively, 'Why don't we find out?'

'That sounds like a challenge.'

'It *is*. Unless, of course . . . '

'I'll give you a fifty-yard head start,' said Maggie, 'and I'll *still* be waiting for you at Pine Ridge.'

Kate felt her competitive streak stir. She thought about her mother's usual mount, a wiry, fourteen-hand chestnut called Blaze. He was a good horse, but had a tendency toward lethargy unless ball spurs were used on him. 'What's at stake?' she asked.

'Your pride,' Maggie answered. Then, without turning, she called, 'Wade! Saddle Sundown for me!'

'*Sundown?*' Kate frowned. Sundown was a fast horse, perhaps the fastest in the entire Carter Ranch remuda. 'What about *your* horse?'

'Sundown *is* my horse,' said Maggie. 'In case you've forgotten, they *all* are.'

Kate realized then that she'd been had; she'd assumed her mother would be riding Blaze, and because of that victory would be easy. But there wasn't much she could do about it now, so all she said was, 'Let's get to it!'

In short order Wade saddled Sundown and led him from the barn. The animal was black as night and sleek as summer grass. He stood fifteen hands, and his long legs and deep chest were built for speed. Maggie took the reins and mounted with quick efficiency. As she settled herself in the saddle, she said, 'Go get your fifty-yard head start, Kathryn. I would say . . . that lodgepole pine with the three stems? That should do it.'

Kate nodded, now well and truly committed. She swung up into her own

39

saddle, gathered her reins and heeled Whiskey into motion. Her heart sank when she realized just how slow he had become in her absence.

The yard fell behind her and the open country leading toward Pine Ridge unfolded ahead. It was an ocean of wind-ruffled sweetgrass dotted with grazing Angus and Hereford cattle, and there, in the distance, a serrated ridge of vast, purple mountains covered in spruce and fir trees, dominated by one ragged peak in particular — Eagle's Nest. It was magnificent country, the complete opposite of what she'd grown used to in St Louis, and seeing it again, *really* seeing it, made her appreciate it all the more.

Then she passed the three-stemmed lodgepole pine, and glancing over one shoulder, saw her mother kick Sundown into a gallop.

'*Come on, Whiskey!*' Kate said, using her heels on the mottled gray. 'Let's show her what we're made of!'

Whiskey broke into a reluctant run,

and beneath them the land dropped into a broad, flat valley. About half a mile to the southeast, a gentle slope led toward her destination, a ridge stippled with ponderosa pine. But even though Kate knew for sure that she was going to lose this race, she realized also that she didn't really care. As far as she was concerned, she had already won something far more precious — the chance to smell this good, clean Montana air again, to feel the warm wind on her face: to watch sheep's wool clouds chase each other across a sky that was bluer than salt water.

She chanced another glance over her shoulder and was startled by just how quickly her mother had closed the gap between them.

'*Come on, Whiskey! Come on!*'

To her surprise Whiskey gave of his best and held nothing back; she knew that instinctively. Old he might be, but he was still game enough to give the younger, faster Sundown a run for his money.

Ahead Pine Ridge drew closer, and beneath them the land began to rise toward its timbered summit. Fleetingly Kate thought she might actually win this race after all, or at least come a respectably close second — but then Whiskey stumbled, recovered . . . and in the same moment Maggie overtook her and Sundown climbed the ridge with effortless, ground-eating strides.

Kate's lips compressed and she thought, *She's never going to let me live this down. But do you know something, Mother? I don't care.*

Maggie was waiting for them when they finally topped out.

Kate, shoulders heaving as she fought to regain her breath, said, 'All right — you . . . proved your point.'

'I didn't *have* a point,' Maggie responded, reaching forward to stroke Sundown's glistening neck. 'It was no more than a horse race. But if you carry away with you a new perspective, so much the better. It could be that knowing when you don't stand a chance is a valuable lesson.'

'You're saying I should know my limitations?'

'On the contrary, Kathryn. I'm saying that you should understand that life doesn't wait for anyone. You have to seize opportunities when they come along.'

'And William Sinclair is my opportunity?'

'He is — and a very fine one, as near as I can see. But William Sinclair is not the only opportunity in your life. There's this place.'

Kate frowned. 'The ranch? But that's yours!'

'Of course. But I won't always be here. And I will rest easier knowing it's in good hands.'

'Ned — '

'Ned,' Maggie cut in, 'has already made his choice. He has chosen a life of debauchery with that saloon owner, Georgia Lamb.'

'I'd hardly call it debauchery.'

'And what would you know of it?'

'I know enough not to assume the worst just because Georgia Lamb owns a saloon. Were it any other business, you would call her exactly that — a businesswoman, like yourself.'

'How little you know of such matters.'

'And how close-minded you've become since Father died,' Kate bit back. 'Does it not even occur to you that Ned might have feelings for Georgia Lamb that go beyond the physical? And that she might have similar feelings for *him*?'

'Is such a thing even *possible* for a woman like that?'

'You're obviously not open to the idea.'

'That woman is a distraction,' Maggie said firmly. 'She has and will continue to distract Ned from his responsibilities closer to home.'

'And because of that, you think I should take over the running of the ranch?'

'Eventually, yes. Is that so bad?'

'I've never really considered it. I always thought — '

'That I'd always be here? I won't, you know.'

'Actually, I was going to say that I never thought you'd trust the ranch to anyone else.'

'Then you should be flattered.'

'I am.'

'But . . . ?'

Kate cut her gaze away to Eagle's Nest, its tip shrouded in low cloud. Then: 'Why not just wait and see what happens? If you're right, then Ned's infatuation with Georgia will soon wear off. If you're wrong, and it really *is* love, then you may need to reconsider your feelings toward Georgia . . . especially if she becomes a daughter-in-law.'

Maggie stiffened. 'If that was a joke, it was in extremely poor taste.'

'It wasn't. But to use your own analogy, Mother, it may be that Georgia Lamb is an *opportunity* herself. An opportunity for Ned to acquire some . . . maturity.'

But she knew Maggie would never see it that way. To her, as she had said,

Georgia Lamb was a distraction — and distraction was the last thing Ned needed, if he were ever to become a man.

'Your horse looks winded,' Maggie said, once again changing the subject.

'Give me one month with Whiskey,' Kate replied, 'and I'll bet a lot more than my pride that you'll never catch me.'

Maggie had not expected that, and in that instant she saw in Kate a mirror image of herself, as perhaps she would have been had life not left her so damaged.

'One month it is,' she said softly. Then she rode back down to the ranch.

3

Kate spent the rest of the morning exploring the ranch and reliving old memories. At around forty thousand acres, the C.A. Carter might not be the largest spread in the state, but it certainly had one of the finest reputations. At its height, her parents had run upwards of three thousand cows on its rolling pastures, together with an appropriate number of bulls and horses. Often she and Ned had accompanied the men on hunting trips into the high country, where there were sizeable populations of elk, mule deer, whitetail deer and antelope.

It was heading for noon when she came to the fence. It was an ugly thing and she took an immediate dislike to it. She believed firmly that range was meant to be free, not divided by wire and wood. And wire, in particular — these weather-tarnished double strands into

47

which were locked cruelly sharp barbs — she found most offensive of all.

One of the few topics her mother had discussed with her at any length was Cyrus McCall's decision to string wire across a portion of his property, effectively stopping Carter cattle from reaching water they had always previously been free to use. The water was still available — even McCall wasn't mean enough to fence *that* off — but with the wire strung, the Carter stock now had to make an arduous two-mile detour before they could reach it.

Rightly or wrongly, Maggie had also taken the stringing of the wire as an unspoken accusation. To her it said, *The rustlers regularly cross your property, Maggie Carter. I guess that means you must be in cahoots with 'em.*

Whether or not Cyrus McCall really believed that — whether or not the thought had even crossed his *mind* — was immaterial. That was the way Maggie had taken it.

For a moment then Kate saw just

what a responsibility her mother bore. A ranch could be demanding even in the best of times. But for a woman alone . . .

But it didn't have to be that way. Ned *was* there to help shoulder the burden, no matter what her mother might think to the contrary. To give him a little trust and responsibility when it came to its running would do them *both* good. But Maggie would never do that. To her, Ned was a disappointment. Worse, Ned knew as much, though Maggie had never come right out and said so. She'd never had to. The very fact that she refused to trust him with anything but the most mundane ranch-tasks told him just how weak-willed and easily led she considered him to be.

Neither did it help that Ned had never had the drive or ambition of his parents. Shy and good-looking — at least before the accident — it seemed to Kate that he had always struggled with the person he was. And when their father died, Ned had suddenly realized that he was never now going to get the chance to show Charlie Carter just what he could amount to. He'd become sullen and uncommunicative, and taken to spending more and more time at Georgia Lamb's saloon.

That was where he'd met Molly Richfield.

Neither Maggie nor Kate had ever known for sure whether Ned had taken up with Molly because he had genuine feelings for her, or because he'd simply wanted to spite his mother, and going with a saloon girl had been a good way to do it. Whichever, there was no denying that Molly had made him feel better about himself. More importantly, she made him feel that he was at least the equal of his friend, Val McCall, and that was something Ned had wanted above all else — to be like his oldest and best friend.

Kate's face shadowed, because what came next was as ugly as the barbed wire that had caused her to draw rein in the first place.

Half-drunk one evening, Ned had gotten it into his head that Val was trying to steal Molly away from him. He'd watched Val and Molly talking together up at the bar, talking and *laughing* together, and suddenly, something inside him had just . . . snapped.

The way she'd heard it told afterwards, Ned had grabbed the bottle from which he'd been drinking, and holding it by the neck, smashed it against the edge of his table. Then he'd advanced on Val and Molly, telling Val to get away from his woman. But Ned was literally stumbling-drunk by then, and somehow he'd tripped over his own feet and gone down — right onto the jagged end of the bottle.

The accident had left Ned badly scarred, and that, more than anything, had shattered whatever small measure of confidence he'd had. Worse, it lost him his best friend. And even though Molly Richfield had stayed with him, he felt she only did so out of pity.

Perhaps he was right. But Kate

couldn't find it in her heart to hate the girl for running off with a drummer. She had a feeling that Ned had driven her away with the mixture of self-pity and self-loathing he fueled with cheap whiskey.

She was just about to gather rein and ride on when she heard the approaching *thrub* of horse-hooves on the far side of the rise. Even as she straightened up and turned at the waist, a magnificent paint mustang charged over the ridge with cream-colored mane flying, and seeing her, quickly veered off toward the south.

A moment later a rider came surging in pursuit of the animal, lariat spinning overhead and ready to throw. Kate recognized him immediately: Val McCall. Intent as he was on his quarry, however, he couldn't fail to notice her there, and reaching a decision, quickly shortened rein to bring his horse to a ground-gouging halt before her, allowing the paint mare — mostly white, but with rounded chestnut patches — to vanish into a stand of firs.

'Well, look who's all growed up!' he greeted, broad shoulders rising and falling as he caught his breath following the chase. Then, indicating the direction in which the mare had just disappeared, 'Been chasin' that critter off an' on for the better part of two years. Almost got her this time.'

She'd known Val since childhood, and could still see in him the boy she'd grown up with. But his features had sharpened a little with age, and it suited him — even with the fading bruises he'd picked up during his fight with the Excelsior Aces still visible. He was an even six feet out of the saddle, with a muscular build that his checked shirt and chap-covered denims couldn't disguise. And when he grinned, it made butterflies dance inside her, and she couldn't decide if that was a good thing or a bad one.

'Some things are just meant to be free,' she said guardedly.

Val coiled his lariat and slung it over

the horn of his saddle. 'She's mine,' he said. 'She just don't know it yet.' Then, cocking his head: 'Say, didn't I see you at the jubilee celebration a few days ago?'

'I'm surprised you saw anything at all, Val McCall,' she replied. 'At the time, two rather large men seemed intent on improving your appearance.'

Val grinned, teeth showing white and even. 'You know, Kate Carter, the first time I laid eyes on you, you was naked as a jaybird. Your mother had you standin' in a wash-pan, scrubbin' dried mud off you. Scared my horse so bad he wouldn't eat for a week. Didn't do me no good, either.'

'I assure you, neither you nor your horse need fear further distress,' she replied. 'My mother's lack of deportment twenty years ago just proves one thing — that we didn't have time for modesty back then. Now, if you don't mind, I'll be moving along. The day is too engaging to waste even a second of it . . . and I daresay you want to go in pursuit of 'your' mare.'

'She's waited this long,' he replied easily. 'She can wait a while longer, I reckon. But . . . '

When he said no more, she prompted him with a, 'Yes?'

'Look, Kate. I know you're a woman of the world now, full of education an' dinner parties an' dudes with slick hair. Me, I think that's too bad, 'cause I liked you a whole lot better when you didn't have all them airs and graces. But forget all that for one second. I got somethin' brand new to show you.'

She arched a brow. 'Now, what could *you* possibly have to show *me*?'

'Just get off your high-horse and follow me,' he replied. 'An' if it ain't the most beautiful thing you ever saw, I'll . . . I'll eat dried mud. My word on it.'

He turned his horse, then reined in again when she stayed where she was. 'Well, you comin' or what?'

She wanted to tell him no, she had better things to do than indulge him and his mysterious ways. But she knew that wasn't true at all. He had piqued her curiosity, and no one could have been more surprised by that than she was herself.

'How am I to get around this fence you McCalls so kindly put up?'

'Hell, it ain't but more'n forty-five inches. Even Whiskey there can clear *that*.'

'Are you suggesting I make him *jump* it?'

'Afraid he can't?' he countered. 'Or maybe that *you* can't?'

Abruptly he pushed his horse back a little closer. 'If you fall,' he said, and all at once there was nothing in him but absolute sincerity, 'I'll be there to pick you up.'

She should have resented the implication. Instead it did something to make her realize that she was a woman and he was a man, and that having someone there to pick you up if you should ever fall was not necessarily a bad thing.

'Kate?' he prompted.

Her eyelids fluttered. 'What?' And then, impulsively, 'Oh, yes. Very well, Val McCall. I'll show you what Whiskey can do.'

She turned the mottled gray and cantered back the way she'd come, determined to give him the best head-start she could. Still, she knew horses had an instinctive hatred of wire, and would sooner jump a board or rail fence any day.

She turned again to face the fence. Here and there a couple of fence posts had begun to sag, and the top strands of wire between them had dipped accordingly. It wasn't much of an advantage, but it was one she determined to use to the full. Focusing on a section where the top wire hung especially low, she reached down to stroke the horse's neck and whispered, 'Come on, Whiskey. You can *do* this. I *know* you can.'

Gathering her nerve, she touched her heels to Whiskey and he lurched into a run. The fence came rushing toward them, and as it did so she knew a brief moment of regret — that she should not have forced such a jump on the animal.

But then Whiskey's forelegs came up, Kate felt herself tilting back in the saddle, and for an instant then they were sailing through the air, both of them, and she was filled with nothing save a wild surge of exhilaration.

Whiskey cleared the fence — just — and came down without breaking stride. She wanted to reach down and hug his neck and tell him how clever he was, but because Val was watching she did nothing of that, merely drew rein when she came alongside him, as if she and Whiskey did this kind of thing all the time.

'Thank you for your offer to pick me up,' she said. 'But as you can see, that was *not* necessary.'

He looked at her in a strange, deep way before finally nodding. 'Well, the offer stands,' he replied. 'You ever need it, I'll be there.'

For an instant everything else in her

was forgotten. Then, to break the moment, she said, 'Well . . . lead on.'

He did so. He led her back over the rise and through pastureland speckled with breeze-blown asters, poppies, lilies and orchids, and she had the craziest feeling that they were the last two people left on earth, a new Adam and Eve for a new century that was now less than five years away.

Ahead there stretched a vast forest of mixed hemlock, ash and elder. They entered the timber and she shivered a little with the chill, for sunlight barely penetrated the intertwined boughs overhead, and there existed only a mossy kind of twilight. In the far distance she saw a flare of sunlight where the trees thinned, and it was toward this light that he led her.

'Just where are you taking me?' she asked after a while, to break the near-silence.

'Remember Wright's Mill?' he answered. 'That valley we sometimes played in as kids?'

59

'What about it?'

'You'll see,' he said.

A few minutes later the trees thinned and they climbed a steep hill until, topping out, she finally saw what had so entranced him.

A broad saddle of land spilled away below them, rising on the far side toward another belt of timber . . . and for the first time in memory the valley itself was teeming with buffalo.

She caught her breath, for nothing could have prepared her for such a majestic sight. There must have been . . . yes, seven or eight hundred of them down there, dams with calves trailing behind them, bulls flicking their tails to dislodge pests while others rolled in shallow depressions to rid themselves of ticks and lice. An especially large bull wandered around the edges of the herd, as if keeping watch, while younger, feistier bulls bellowed and roared challenges and rubbed their horns against such scant timber as there was.

'Well, what do you think of that,

Kate?' Val asked at last. 'Nothin' like it in St. Louis, I reckon.'

It was all she could do to tear her gaze away from the herd. 'I can't dispute that.'

'See how them bulls're mixin' with the dams?' he said with a gesture. 'They don't hardly ever do that, but it's breedin' season right now, so they're eyein' up potential mates. See that big feller down there, way he's stickin' extra-close to that female? He's tryin' to keep her from seein' the competition! Wants her all to himself, see?'

'Selfish,' she said. 'Like all men.'

'Sounds to me like you been seein' the wrong men,' he replied mildly.

'It is my understanding,' she said, 'that once the bull has had what he wants, he has nothing more to do with the dam, and plays no part in the rearing of their offspring.'

'You sayin' I won't be a good father to *our* children?' he challenged, and she couldn't tell if he was teasing or if he really meant it.

She felt her cheeks heat again. 'You're very sure of yourself,' she said, and realized that a short time earlier her mother had more or less said exactly the same thing about her.

'Billy Broken Hand told me about them,' he went on, naming a local half-breed Crow Indian who supplied horses for Big Sky and other neighboring ranches.

'Billy Broken Hand? Does he still live around here?'

'Sure. He says the buffalo migrated south from the border, the way it used to be before their hides became so popular back east.'

She couldn't resist what she said next. 'I'm surprised the McCalls aren't stringing barbed wire even as we speak.'

His mood darkened at that. 'McCalls hate wire as much as anyone, Kate, but when you're losin' cows there ain't much choice. Nothin' agin your ma, mind. But them rustlers always drive McCall stock across Carter land.'

'And I suppose — '

'Don't suppose nothin', Kate. Charlie Carter was top of the heap. Pa always said there was no better man in the territory. But when he passed on . . .'

' . . . everything turned sour,' she said, thinking of Ned. 'I know.'

'Now, I didn't say that.'

'You didn't have to. But a woman with no one but a stargazing son to help her has no business running a ranch. Am I right?'

He heeled his horse closer, and took hold of Whiskey's cheek strap. 'Now you hold up. Everyone knows Maggie Carter's got sand. Lord knows, she's got her hands full. And Ned . . . well, he'll . . . he'll come to his senses again, one of these days. I'm gonna see to it.'

'Well, you see to it, Val McCall. And thank you for that.' His nearness had a strange, fluttery effect upon her, an effect William Sinclair had never managed to inspire, and struggling to get her feelings back under control, she nodded toward the buffalo. 'You were right. This was indeed something brand new.'

He was pleased. 'Say, why don't we go down to Wright's Mill again, like we used to? I ain't been there myself in a — '

But she was her mother's daughter. Time was wasting. 'No, thank you,' she said formally. And then she turned her mount and rode away, feeling his eyes on her back even long after she was out of his sight.

4

That afternoon, Maggie tried to concentrate on ranch business. As she transferred numbers from her tally pad and that of Wade Palmer to her permanent record, she saw that, despite everything, it had been a good year. If the coming winter was mild — as everyone seemed to be predicting — it would almost guarantee a banner year for the C.A. Carter.

Then why did she feel so . . . so *flat?* What was it in her that made it impossible for her to feel even a glimmer of pride in her achievements; that it was always necessary for her to prove herself in what was and likely always would be a man's world?

Before she could consider the matter further — a worthless pastime anyway, for she had done so many times in the past and never yet found a satisfactory answer — there came a soft rapping at the door.

'Come in, Kathryn,' she called.

Kate came inside. 'How did you know it was me?' she asked.

Maggie set her pen aside, pinched the tired flesh at the bridge of her short nose. 'For one thing, only you and Hester would dare knock on my door,' she replied, naming their housekeeper. 'And your touch is more delicate than hers.'

Kate glanced around.

After her father died, her mother had closed off their bedroom and moved the bare essentials — a desk, a single bed, a dresser and two chairs — to this small, confining room at the end of the first floor hallway. It was where she handled ranch business and spent such free time as she allowed herself, and to which few were ever invited.

'What do you want, anyway?' asked Maggie. 'I thought you'd be out limbering up your father's horse . . . unless, of course, you've had a change of heart about our return match?'

'The only change I foresee is the look on your face when you and that jackrabbit Sundown eat my dust.'

For an instant Maggie almost smiled. But *almost* was as close as she ever came to that particular expression. 'Confidence is one thing,' she said. '*Over*-confidence is something else entirely.'

'Think what you may,' Kate said sweetly, 'while you strive for his hindquarters.'

Maggie sighed. 'I ask again. What do you want?'

Kate's humor faded. She said quickly, 'I've come to tell you that I've decided not to accept William's proposal of marriage. And before you say anything — '

'What makes you think I have anything to *say*?'

'Because you're *you*, Mother.'

'Very well. So you have made your choice. May I ask what finally decided you?'

'Nothing in particular,' Kate lied.

'Then does it follow that you have opted instead to take over the ranch whenever I choose to hand it to you?'

'I . . . I still don't know about that. The ranch is as much Ned's birthright as mine — more so, since he's the elder child.'

'But . . . ?'

'But I would gladly accept the responsibility of running the ranch alongside him.'

'Then you may well find that you end up doing the work of two. Do you know where he is right now?'

'No.'

'Neither do I, though I can guess. He is gone more often than he's here, sometimes for a day or more, sometimes longer. Does that strike you as the actions of a man with any commitment to the ranch he will one day inherit?'

'It's as I said, Mother — '

'Ned is Ned, yes, I know. But a man's nature should not be used as an excuse.'

'He'll come round, eventually. I know he will.' Then, to change the subject, 'I happened upon Val McCall this afternoon.'

She didn't miss the way her mother stiffened at the name.

'He was trying to run down a paint mustang,' she continued quickly. 'Without much success, it has to be said. I surmise that seeing me gave him as good an excuse as any to quit.' She hesitated a moment, then said, 'He showed me a place down near Wright's Mill that was truly beautiful.'

'Did he, now?' Abruptly Maggie closed her books. 'Kathryn, Val McCall is nothing but trouble. Ask your brother.'

'You're really talking about Molly Richfield, aren't you?'

'She set her cap for young McCall and used your brother to get to him. She made Ned feel as if he meant something to her, when all the time he was just a means to an end. Then, when she had no further need of him, she cut him off in a blink, and left him marked for life.'

'Val McCall didn't scar Ned's face with that bottle.'

'But he was with Molly when Ned

came upon them.'

'There was nothing going on. You *know* there wasn't! Val and Molly were just talking. Ned was drunk. He fell and gashed his own face.'

'Valentine McCall was Ned's friend. He should have looked out for him.'

'If you call Val arrogant, if you tell me he's plain full of himself, I'll give you no argument. But show me a man worthy of a second look who wasn't like that. I don't believe for one moment that Val set out to hurt Ned. Even *you* said Val tried to make it up to him, afterward.'

'All I'm *saying*,' Maggie said deliberately, 'is stay away from Val McCall. Nothing's going to change what's born bad.'

Kate looked at her mother as if she were a stranger. Maggie told herself it meant nothing, but she found it curiously unsettling.

'Father and the McCalls were fast friends,' said the girl. 'What happened?'

'Your father was a gentle man. A kind

man. And too soft at times. And back then, there were no fences.'

'No one was stealing cattle then.'

'Just steer clear,' insisted Maggie. 'For your own good. And let that be an end to it.'

'But — '

'I have nothing more to offer on the matter,' said Maggie, adding meaningfully, 'And neither do *you.*'

* * *

In her bedroom above the saloon, Georgia Lamb and Ned Carter lay side by side, the sheets rumpled around them. Beyond the curtained window, night lay draped across Singletree. In the saloon below, they could hear the sounds of men laughing and talking, the automated tinkling of Georgia's Aeolian player piano, the clink and rattle of bottleneck on glass-rim, the occasional explosion of excitement as someone won a hand of faro or poker.

Their lovemaking had been good

— leastways, for him. Georgia was a good partner, encouraging, supportive. But whether she derived the same level of pleasure from these stolen moments of theirs, he was never quite sure.

At length he rolled out of bed, finger-combed his long brown hair back off his scarred face and started to dress. Georgia watched him for a while, then rose and went, naked, to help him button his shirt and straighten his vest.

'Wish I could stay longer,' said the boy. 'But I been gone from the ranch all day as it is.'

'I know,' she replied. She had a long face and a strong jaw, direct green eyes and soft auburn hair that now spilled around her bare shoulders. At forty, she was sixteen years older than Ned, and more than a whole lifetime wiser in terms of experience. She'd started her working life as a saloon girl — no sex, just there to brighten up the lives of the women-starved men by listening, encouraging them to buy drinks or spend seventy-five cents for a dance. And to their credit, the men had generally behaved themselves, being only too aware just how rare and precious a woman was on the frontier.

Of course, not everyone had been of the same mind. Things could turn violent if a man drank too much or figured he deserved more than just a friendly smile and a little harmless flirting. Georgia herself had known six girls who'd ended up beaten or killed.

But she'd never intended to stay in the business long enough for that to happen to her. She'd earned twelve dollars a week back then and saved ten of them, and as soon as she had money behind her she quit and headed north to the Montana Territory, where she'd heard that miners were earning well and had money to burn. She'd opened up this place, and never looked back.

Falling in love — much less falling in love with someone young enough to be her son — had never figured in her plans. It had just happened. But it was a curious kind of love because it made her happy and yet unhappy all at once. She had no doubt that Ned Carter meant all the flowery things he told her, and she found his attention flattering. But there was an ever-present element of doubt there, too, for what did he really know of life and love? He was twenty-five, yes — but only in years. Emotionally he was still a child — worse, a petulant one, on occasion.

'But now you need to get going,' she continued gently. 'And I need to get back to running my business. Besides, I don't need your mother gunning for me.'

Ned's mouth twisted. 'It's none of her business who I spend time with.'

'Something tells me it *is*.'

His expression flattened out. 'Oh, she pushed and prodded my father sure enough, but I'm damned if I'll let her run my life the same way.'

He might have said more, but she chose that moment to put a finger on his lips to silence him.

It didn't work.

'You don't believe me, do you?' he asked.

'I never said that.'

'You didn't have to. You *know* how much of a man I am.'

'Sure I do, Ned. I never said any different.'

'But the way you look at me sometimes, like — '

'Like what?'

'Like I'm just a kid. I'm *not*.'

'You are,' she said. 'Compared to me.'

He looked at her for a long, baffled moment. 'Is that what's bothering you?' he asked, as if it could really be that simple.

She shrugged. 'Your mother and I are of an age.'

'What's that got to do with anything?'

Georgia knew what Maggie thought of her, well enough. She'd convinced herself that Georgia was a monster, a cradle-snatcher, intent on filling her son with liquor and robbing him of innocence and ambition both. And by so doing she was destroying any future the C.A. Carter Ranch could expect.

Georgia tried to be philosophical about it. Maybe that was the only way a woman like Maggie Carter *could* think: to always see the bad, and never the good. She didn't really understand that love could sometimes be pure, genuine, given freely and with no expectation of anything in return.

In that moment Georgia felt sorry for Maggie Carter. Very sorry indeed.

'I asked you a question,' Ned persisted. 'What's that got to do with anything?'

'Nothing, I guess,' she sighed.

Impulsively he tried to kiss her, believing that the rougher he was, the more manly he would appear to her. But as much as she loved him, she hated it when he turned rough and surly. She turned her head, so that his mouth brushed her cheek and not her lips.

'Go home, Ned,' she told him.

'*Now* what have I done?'

For a moment she was going to say

nothing. Instead she said, 'Sooner or later you *will* stand on your own two feet. For your sake, I hope it's sooner. Then you'll realize that being a man isn't so much about what you can take by force.'

He was immediately chastened. 'I'm sorry,' he said, and there it was again, she thought; that plaintive whine she had come to hate. 'Please,' he went on, 'I *would* like to stay.'

'I know,' she said. 'But off with you. Go on — *scat!*'

He backed away from her, wanting to understand the way things really were but too immature to do so. He picked up his hat and slapped it on, then said goodnight and left.

★ ★ ★

He thought about Georgia all the way home. Was he really the boy she seemed to think he was? God, he was a man full-grown! And yet here he was, still living in his mother's shadow, still taking her orders, no closer to standing up for himself now than he'd ever been.

He hated it. He hated what he saw in the mirror every day, and not just because of the scars, but what lay beneath them and in back of his eyes — a weak-willed kid who'd never grown up — who'd never been given the *chance* to grow up.

One day, he thought, he'd show everyone. And if all went the way he hoped it would, that day would come real soon. But then he realized just how long he'd been promising himself that, and he heard the hollowness of it and knew he was too weak even to make good on a promise made to no one but himself.

The ranch came into sight, a silhouette against the purple, star-sprinkled sky. One solitary light burned smoky yellow at the window of his mother's room. He scowled as he discerned her shadow, sitting in a chair before the window.

He saw to his horse, then entered the

house and went, almost reluctantly, upstairs. He had only been into his mother's room on a handful of occasions, and he hated it in there. If she wanted to see him now, if that's why she had waited up, she was going to be out of luck. He'd vanish into his room and whatever she wanted would have to wait till morning.

Ned reached the head of the stairs and turned hurriedly toward his own room, but he wasn't quick enough.

'Ned.'

The sound of his mother's voice froze him.

'Ned,' she called again. 'Come here.'

He turned. Her door stood ajar, lamplight forming a thin oblong on the floral carpet. He took off his hat and reluctantly went as far as the doorframe.

'What is it, Ma?'

She was looking up at him from behind her desk, her shadow, thrown by the lantern to her left, looming large on the wall behind her. 'I have a Stock

Growers meeting to attend first thing in the morning,' she said, 'and in case it's slipped your mind, we have three hundred head to move onto the north range at first light. You know we're short-handed, and it'll take every man we can spare. And yet still you insist on spending half the night — ' She wanted to say *fornicating*, but couldn't bring herself to use such a word. ' — gallivanting,' she finished.

He tried to tell himself that he shrugged, but it was more akin to a squirm, and he hated himself for that, too. 'I'll be the first one in the saddle come daylight.'

'Perhaps you will,' she allowed. 'But you'll be angry and mean and spitting hatred for everything that crosses your path. And why? Because you spent half the night with a harlot who saps all your energy.'

'That's crazy — '

'Is it?' she countered. 'She breaks your will and bridles your ambition — and you run with blinders.'

He planted himself a little firmer. 'I see better than you give me credit for, Ma. Where I've been tonight ain't nobody's business but mine. All you need to know is I've been where I *want* to be. Where I can find some peace. Where I really come to life, and feel like I count for something!'

Maggie heard him out, her expression impassive. 'Oh, you *are* somebody,' she said. 'Somebody who leaves his ten dollars on a dusty dresser. Somebody who slinks down back stairs into an alley.'

He looked down at her, his expression mirroring the pity Georgia felt for her. 'You've got it wrong,' he said. 'There's no money changes hands. No back stairs.'

'It's *always* that way,' she assured him. 'You just allow the intoxication of cheap perfume to convince you otherwise.'

'At least I'm alive,' he said.

'Oh? And what's *that* supposed to mean?'

'It means I'm going *out*, Ma, I'm meeting folks, making friends and doing something with my life.'

'And I'm not?'

His temper up, he came deeper into the room. 'When Pa died you shut yourself away in this . . . this mausoleum!' He looked around, a little wildly now, until his eyes found a box sitting on the dresser. 'Well,' he continued, 'that's not for me. I don't want it, and I won't have it! You want me to act like just another one of your possessions, you're going have to lock *me* up in a box!'

So saying, he swept the box off the dresser. As it hit the floor the lid came off and a collection of pictures and letters fanned out across the carpet, along with an old cap-and-ball Navy Colt.

Furious, Maggie sprang up. '*Ned!* Those letters are from your grandmother!'

'Yes,' he said. 'And they're older than me! But what's this?'

He scooped up the Colt.

Maggie's face closed up and her voice turned flat. 'Just an old gun.'

'Who did it belong to? My grandfather?'

'Yes. He carried that at Gettysburg.'

He dropped the weapon onto the desk. She flinched at the clatter it made. But Ned didn't notice. Instead he snatched up a handful of daguerreotypes.

'Who *are* these people?' he asked. 'Who's this?'

'Your grandmother.'

'And him?'

'My father.'

'And this one?'

Maggie stared at the picture in his hand. It showed a man with regular features, dark eyes, a once-broken nose, a crooked mouth firmed now into a sober line. Emotions warred in her expression. Then she tore her gaze from the image.

'Who's he?' he demanded.

'He was . . . my mother's husband.

After my father died.'

'These people,' he said, 'they're strangers, names on headstones, that's all. What's real for you died thirty years ago!'

'What's real for me is here! What your father built from *nothing!* And now it's yours to make ever *bigger!*' She came around the desk. 'Don't be corrupted by the likes of Molly Richfield. She was desperate, pathetic, a *nobody!* She brought you to your knees, and Georgia Lamb is like to finish you once and for all. But Carter Ranch makes you *somebody*, Ned. It gives you the chance to be a man — a man, like your father!'

'I *am* somebody, Ma,' he told her. 'Not much, I know, leastways not by your lights. But at least with Georgia I know how it feels to be wanted.'

He turned and stormed out, slamming the door behind him. Maggie stared after him for a few moments, then bent and gathered up all the papers and put them back into the box.

The last thing she put away was the gun . . . and when she handled it she did so with something approaching reverence.

5

At first Maggie didn't hear the plaintive bellowing. She was, as ever, preoccupied with her troubled thoughts, chief among them the Stock Growers Association meeting she was now on her way to attend.

Then the sound intruded upon her, and all else was suddenly thrust aside as she drew rein and sat a little straighter in her saddle, trying to pinpoint the direction from which the sound was coming.

After a few seconds she set heels to Sundown and he took her up and over the crest of a rise, where she reined down sharply at the sight that confronted her.

A line of barbed wire ran southeast to northwest across the wooded hollow below. A yearling calf had become entangled in it, while the bellowing mother could do no more than stand close by and watch as the calf's struggles grew increasingly feeble.

Maggie sent her horse down slope. The cow watched her come through dark, fluid eyes. Even before Sundown came to a halt, Maggie threw herself from the saddle. Leaving the horse ground-hitched, she ran across to the calf and surveyed its predicament. A tiny sound that could have been a moan escaped her. The more it had struggled to get free, the more the calf had become hopelessly entangled in the wire. Worse, the barbs had torn the animal's skin in numerous places and there was blood everywhere. The creature was more or less bled out.

Which meant there could be no saving it.

Maggie stepped back. The calf looked up at her through glazing eyes. She tipped her head back, looked up at the vast blue bowl of sky above her, then drew a breath and turned to her saddlebags, in which she kept the snake-gun she always carried when travelling to and from town.

Behind her, the cow bellowed again, almost as if sensing what must come next.

Steeling herself, Maggie took the gun out, drew back the hammer and pointed it at the calf.

The calf blinked once, and then Maggie pulled the trigger.

The shot echoed for what seemed like a very long time.

Maggie stood there, looking down through a shifting gauze of gun smoke. The calf lay still now, no longer struggling, but it was scant consolation. Her mouth twitched, suddenly the calf was obscured by something other than gun smoke, and then she swiped a hand across her face, the move quick, irritable, angry. There could be no room for tears in her life now. Not ever again.

'Pity,' said someone behind her.

She jumped, straightened and turned to see a tall, narrow-hipped man sitting a bay horse a few yards away. How he'd gotten so close without her sensing him there she couldn't even imagine.

Instinctively she brought up the gun. Seeing that, the newcomer hurriedly raised his free hand, palm out. 'Whoa, there, ma'am. I'm not the enemy. Just heard the shot is all, came to have a look and see who fired it.'

He was somewhere in his late thirties, with a long face and a trimmed red beard. His beady blue eyes moved beyond her to the dead calf, its mother now nosing at the body, as if convinced it was only sleeping and needed nothing more than waking up. 'Wire's mean,' he murmured. 'Your animal, ma'am?'

Maggie hesitated a moment more, then let the gun drop back to her side. 'It is,' she allowed. 'You work for McCall?'

'No, ma'am.'

'Right now it's a good thing that you don't.'

'I was just riding through,' he continued, 'trying to find a way around

89

this here wire.' He dismounted suddenly, his movements easy, graceful. He slid a large knife from his belt and busied himself cutting the dead calf free. 'Name's Bateman, ma'am. Caleb Bateman.' He stopped, gave her a closer scrutiny. 'Say, you wouldn't be Mrs. Carter, would you? Ned's mother?'

'I'm Margaret Carter, yes,' she replied. 'You know Ned?'

'Met him a while back — good man. So I know a little of the vinegar between the Carters and the McCalls. Now I see *why*.' He finished his grisly chore, straightened back to his full six feet two. He wore range clothes — check shirt, well-worn denims and shotgun chaps, unbuckled now, so that they made a heavy, rubbery sound when he moved. He also wore a sidearm high on his left hip, a big Smith & Wesson Russian in .44 caliber. 'Don't know how you put up with it, Mrs. Carter,' he went on. 'No call for fences out here. This is open range, free grazing land.'

'Not according to Cyrus McCall.'

'Well, McCall might pack a lot of sand in these parts, but that don't make him right, leastways not this time. A man — even a woman, comes to that — shouldn't have to — '

'Too many words, Mr. Bateman,' she interrupted. 'Too many *ifs* and *buts* and *shoulds*. Men talk a good game, but in my experience, that's *all* they do.'

For a moment it looked as if Bateman might dispute that, but instead he merely nodded. 'Could be you got somethin' there, Mrs. Carter. Talk's cheap, and thin as paper. It's actions that speak louder.' He slapped the gun at his hip, then indicated the calf. 'Maybe this is the final straw,' he suggested. 'Maybe it's time you *took* action.'

Without waiting for a response, he touched his fingers to the curled brim of his tobacco-brown Stetson and remounted.

'Ma'am,' he said — and rode away.

★ ★ ★

In town, ranch owners from miles around were arriving for the Stock Growers quarterly meeting. As wagons were stalled and saddle horses hitched or turned out in the public corral, ranchers called greetings to each other and then made for Georgia Lamb's saloon. Spirits were high, for the year had been a good one. Indeed, the only downside had been the rustling, which seemed to have hit Cyrus McCall's Big Sky hardest of all.

Waiting for them on the porch outside the saloon was Granville Stuart, a tall, bleak-looking man in black, who ran the Association on behalf of its members. Stuart's handshake was firm as he greeted Cyrus and nodded to the McCall foreman, Gil Farrow.

McCall himself was a powerful-looking man, not tall — a little under six feet — but one who exuded strength and force. He was in his late fifties now, and running to fat, but his gaze was still sharp and direct, his voice still the low, vaguely-threatening rasp of gravel it had always been. He seldom smiled — his life had been such a testing one that he'd never seen much to smile about — but he was a fair man and one well-liked.

Now Granville Stuart said, 'Once more unto the breach, eh, Cyrus?'

McCall's response was little more than a grunt. His attention had been taken by the arrival of Maggie Carter, and as she reined it before the hitch rack, he reached up one gnarled hand to scratch thoughtfully at his pure-white beard.

McCall had always liked and respected Charlie Carter, but likewise had always suspected that Maggie wore the pants in their relationship. He had old-fashioned ideas about women, and though he admired her courage, he felt that she'd taken on too much following Charlie's death. But even he understood that Maggie had little choice in the matter. Maggie's boy, Ned . . . well, he had little time for that one. 'Fact, he'd been relieved when Ned had quarreled with Val and ended their long-time friendship. He'd always been worried that Ned's weak, irresponsible nature might rub off on his son.

Maggie dismounted, a handsome woman despite the rough trail clothes she wore. She looped her reins at the rack, then stepped up onto the boardwalk and went straight into the saloon without a glance in Cyrus's direction.

Suddenly Granville Stuart seemed ill at ease, knowing that the grudge Maggie carried for Cyrus was likely to dominate what might otherwise be a cordial gathering. 'Shall we, uh, go in, Cyrus?'

Cyrus didn't nod, didn't speak. He just brushed past the Association man and went inside with Gil Farrow following like a shadow.

The saloon had been closed for the duration of the meeting, as it usually was. Cigarette smoke drifted around the rafters, but no one would be allowed to drink until the meeting was adjourned. Maggie deliberately seated herself at a table to one side of the batwing doors, well away from the other ranchers. She felt no kinship with them, and didn't care who knew it. As Cyrus came inside, the chatter died down until all that could be heard was the fall of his heavy, high-heeled cowman's boots, the musical ring of his jinglebob spurs.

'All right,' said Stuart, when Cyrus and Farrow had taken their seats at a table near the bar. 'I'd say we're ready to start. First of all, I want to thank Georgia again, for allowing us to meet in her hallowed establishment.'

Behind the bar, Georgia shrugged, stunning in a figure-hugging taffeta dress, burgundy with black lace at the plunging neckline. 'Any time, Mr. Stuart. Just know you're all expected to support this 'hallowed establishment' the second the meeting adjourns.'

A ripple of laughter ran through the assembly. As she was speaking Georgia glanced uneasily at Maggie. Maggie pointedly turned away. The move was not lost on Simon Doubleday, who was there to cover the meeting for the *Enterprise*.

Stuart said, 'As you can see, I've invited Judge Blackmer and Simon to sit in today.'

Fat and balding, Judge Blackmer acknowledged the introduction. 'Oh, it's nothing official. I'm just here as a guest.'

'And as always,' added Simon, 'the *Enterprise* will publish an accurate record of what's discussed here today.'

'That'll be a first,' growled McCall.

There was another spatter of laughter, until Stuart nodded toward Sheriff McKenna. 'First order of business, gentlemen, I've asked the sheriff here to bring us all up to date on our, ah, rustling problem.'

The laughter quickly dried up.

McKenna pushed away from the table against which he'd been resting his rump. He was a little rooster of a man, feisty, humorless and dedicated to his job. Though short and slight, only a fool would ever underestimate him; on more than one occasion he'd shown he was utterly fearless. 'As you all know,' he said, 'these rustlers are a cut above the usual thief. They operate mostly at night — but not always. They take a few head here and a few head there, and then just seem to disappear. My deputy and me've combed the area all the way up to the Green Mountain Reservation, and ... nothin'. Indian agent hasn't seen nor heard a thing. About the only good news to date is that they've slowed down since Cyrus McCall strung his wire.'

'Slowed down, sure,' growled McCall. 'But not stopped.'

'Well, like I say, Cyrus, it's a start. If we make it as hard as we can for 'em, maybe they'll move on.'

'And get away with what they've already done here?' asked McCall. 'Not good enough, McKenna. This started here. Ought to finish here, too, else it just becomes someone else's damn' problem — an' it sends out the wrong message.'

McKenna looked at him. 'And what message is that, Cyrus?'

'That we can't take care of our own business,' McCall replied. 'That we're easy pickin's. That kind of word gets out, then they'll come from miles around, every low-life and sharper, every owl-hoot and scavenger.'

'Now, I don't think it's likely to — '

'You know somethin', McKenna? I don't care what you think. I seen it happen before. We got rustlers in these parts. It's our problem and we got to deal with it ourselves — now. And when them rustlers is hangin' high, that sends out a message, too. That if you're plannin' any larceny, you'd best ride wide around Singletree.'

McKenna's narrow face hardened. 'Now see here, Cyrus, as long as I wear this badge, we'll have *law* here, not *lynch* law — '

Judge Blackmer pumped his head. 'The sheriff's right, Cyrus. There'll be no vigilantism in these parts as long as I'm on the county board.'

'Then find 'em and deal with 'em,' McCall growled. 'Or maybe we'll have no choice but to take your *law* into our own hands.'

'He's right, Sheriff,' muttered Asa Hayes. 'All your speechifyin' don't help me none.'

'Nor me,' said John Bascomb. 'Oh, I got sympathy for you, Sheriff. This is a big country, an' there's plenty places for these rustlers to hole up. But they've got to be stopped. Cyrus has been hit hardest of all, it's true. But Big Sky . . . well, Big Sky's *big*. It can afford a few losses every now and then. Me, I can't.'

'I understand how you gentlemen feel,' said McKenna. 'All I can tell us is we're doin' everythin' we can to run these varmints to ground. But it takes time — and there's only me and one deputy to cover an awful lot of ground.'

'What about — '

Before Bascomb could speak further, Maggie got to her feet, the backward scrape of chair legs cutting across the rancher's voice.

'Mr. Stuart,' she said, 'I have a ranch

to run — so if you don't mind, I'll say my piece and then leave.'

Stuart began uncomfortably, 'Well, Maggie, we — '

'Ah, let her speak,' said one of the ranchers.

Maggie took the silence that followed as agreement.

'I imagine you all know why I'm here,' she said. 'It's McCall's wire.'

McCall stirred ponderously like a grizzly coming out of hibernation. 'I don't like fences any more'n you do, Maggie Carter,' he rumbled. 'But I ain't losin' more cows.' His piggy eyes sought and found Stuart. 'Next order of business.'

But Maggie wasn't going to be stopped now.

'I know most all of you think I have no business being here,' she said, 'that by taking over my dead husband's responsibilities I've somehow assumed more than a woman can handle. Well, I might not belong here in your eyes, but I'm damned if I'll cut loose one more bleeding, half-dead cow and not do something about it.'

'Get to the point,' said Cyrus.

'Creek Run's open range, and you know it,' Maggie replied. 'You know I don't have anything to do with your missing cows. Carter Ranch might not be Big Sky, but we've been neighbors long enough for you to know that I'd sooner eat dirt than take anything that's not mine.

'My husband, rest his soul, once said to me that Singletree's Stock Growers Association would set the moral direction for the town. Prove it to me now by doing what's right — take down that wire!'

'Not a hope in hell,' said Cyrus. 'Not as long as we got rustlers. You heard the sheriff. At least it's slowed 'em down.'

'And it's *crippling* me, Cyrus McCall! Because of your wire, I now have to drive my stock an extra two miles to reach water. It takes time and manpower that I can ill afford, and to use your own phrase against you, it sends out the wrong message — that I must be in league with the rustlers because they run *your* stock across *my* land!'

'I never said that.'

'You didn't have to!' She frowned at him, shook her head almost imperceptibly. 'Why do you want to spite me so, Cyrus? I have no desire to change the complexion of this organization. All I want is a little respect and consideration for what is right and fair. So think on this, all of you. If that wire doesn't come down — and *soon* — then I promise you . . . there'll be hell to pay!'

6

Maggie was still in a mood at supper that night. She sat at one end of the long oak table, opposite the empty place that Charlie Carter used to occupy. Nubbs sat to her left, across from Kate and Ned. You could have cut the atmosphere with a blunt knife, and Nubbs — when he did occasionally glance up from his rabbit stew — looked as if he'd sooner be anywhere but where he was right then.

So it was almost a relief when the dogs outside started barking, and they all heard the rattle of a buckboard drawing up outside.

Kate and Ned exchanged a look. Visitors were rare to the C.A. Carter, and as far as they knew, no one was expected. But a few moments later there came a brisk knock at the door.

Hester hurried from the kitchen to

answer it. Outside, on the lantern-lit porch, she found a tall, narrow-flanked man in a well-tailored gray suit and a matching John Bull top hat. He flashed her a winning smile as she looked up into his face, which was long and well-defined.

'Margaret?' he said, doffing his hat. Then, without waiting for a reply: 'It's been a long time, and you don't recognize me, do you?'

Hester shook her head, a little flustered. 'I'm not Mrs. Carter,' she replied. 'Margaret is in the dining room. Please — come in.'

He followed her into the house and through to the dining room, his dark, glittering eyes seemingly everywhere at once. He wore his dusty black hair long, and with a side part. His mustache and goatee were of the same color. As he entered the dining room, he smiled broadly and fondly at the family, his manner effortlessly charming.

'Forgive the intrusion,' he said. 'Margaret? It's been a long time. I'm — '

' — Joshua Carter,' Maggie finished, rising to her feet. 'Charles's . . . *adventurous* . . . younger brother.'

She did the best she could to hide her surprise at his unexpected arrival, but it did nothing to improve her mood. The last thing she needed right now was Charles's brother, a man she had never liked. Younger than Charles by a decade, he had become a wanderer, gambler and ladies' man who had experienced many reversals of fortune in his turbulent life. More than once his slick manner and agile intelligence had saved him from enemies who would have gladly done him in. Whatever he was doing here now could mean nothing good, of that she was certain.

'I am so sorry,' he said, coming around the table and taking both of her hands in his. 'I didn't hear of Charles's passing until six weeks ago. I've been in South America for over a year, you see. I didn't receive your letter until I returned to Galveston.'

Maggie turned to her children. 'Kate,

Ned . . . you remember your Uncle Joshua?'

It was clear that they hardly remembered him at all, but were too polite to say so.

Joshua reached for and kissed Kate's right hand, then shook with Ned.

'This here,' Maggie continued, 'is Nelson Nubbins.'

Again Joshua extended his hand. Nubbs looked up at him from under his beetle brows, saw enough in his one quick glance to know that he didn't like this man and couldn't trust him, then looked away, refusing to take it.

'You've already met Hester, of course,' Maggie said into the sudden, uncomfortable silence. 'Won't you . . . ah . . . join us?'

'Why, thank you,' he replied, and made to take Charles Carter's seat at the head of the table until Maggie said quickly, 'Over there, if you will.'

As Hester briskly set another place for him beside Nubbs, he sat down, completely at home and apparently oblivious to the searching appraisal of Kate, who was trying to find something of her father in him, and Ned, who was still taking his measure. As soon as a bowl of stew was set before him, he picked up a spoon and began to eat.

'Delicious,' he pronounced. 'You know, I can't tell you how pleasant it is to taste home cooking after so long. Charles must have been very proud of his life here. He was blessed indeed.'

'It wasn't always that way,' said Maggie.

'Oh, I'm well aware of the hardships he — both of you — faced year after year. But having a son to follow in his footsteps, a lovely daughter to make him proud, a woman to comfort and — '

Tired of what was rapidly turning into a speech, Maggie decided that the time had come for a little straight talking. 'Charles Carter deserved better than he got. To be taken in one's prime, having already survived war and the harshness of this land, is out of tune with all that is just. All we can do to

107

honor him is continue to build upon what he started. But enough of the past, Joshua. You're a long way from Galveston. What brings you here now?'

'My brother knew me well,' Joshua replied, addressing them all with a sweeping glance and a wry smile. 'He would be the first to tell you I'm ill at ease unless the sea is at my back. But the sea is a cruel mistress. And I think I'm finally ready to have both feet firmly on the ground.'

Abruptly he raised the glass Hester had just poured for him. 'To land,' he said. 'Solid, dependable . . . forgiving.'

Ned suddenly pushed his chair back and rose. 'I got to be movin',' he said.

His mother glared at him. 'Oh? Moving *where*, exactly?'

'I got friends to see,' he replied shortly. 'Nice to've met you . . . Uncle, ah, Joshua.'

'And I to meet you,' Joshua replied, rising and shaking his hand again. 'I hope to see more of you in the days ahead.'

Ned murmured something noncommittal and left the room.

'Now,' said Joshua, turning back to Maggie and breaking the awkward silence Ned had left behind him, 'where were we?'

*   *   *

Later, after Nubbs had retired to his attic room, and Kate had gone to take one last look at Whiskey before bedtime, Maggie and Joshua retired to the parlor, where Maggie fixed them each a brandy.

As he took his glass, Joshua said, 'You have a beautiful daughter, Margaret. And Ned has become a fine man.'

'Ned . . .' she began. Then: 'Charles's death set him adrift, I'm afraid. He's still searching for something to hold onto.'

'A father figure,' he mused. 'Who's the big mute who refused my hand?'

'Nubbs? Oh, don't mind him. He was here when I first met Charles. He served under Charles in Missouri and

Kansas during the war, and Charles was always the one person he could trust. He's devoted to us, and I trust him with my life.'

Joshua wandered around the room, admiring the furnishings. It was neat and tidy, seldom used but well appointed. As with the dining room, it was traditionally furnished, with French floral wallpaper above a picture rail from which hung a selection of framed landscapes. A rectangular braided rug covered the varnished parquet floor, and unfussy straight drapes hung at the two long windows. There were shelves filled with books, and an impressive collection of long guns in a rack behind the door. He went to them, recognized an old Baker flintlock, a Krag-Jørgensen, a .22 caliber parlor gun, a long-barreled Berthier rifle of the kind still popular in Europe, and an old Whitworth rifle to which was attached a long William Malcolm rifle scope.

'He loved you very much, you know,' he said suddenly.

'What?'

'Charles. There was nothing he wouldn't do for you.'

'He was a good man. This was his favorite room.'

Joshua inclined his head toward the gun rack. 'I can see that. It's a man's room. And those rifles are beautiful.'

Following his gaze, she remarked, 'You know, he never carried a sidearm. He'd had his fill of watching men die. Yet he saw art in their form. He was drawn to the feel of long guns, felt secure with them.' Her eyes found his, suddenly. 'A complicated man, your brother.'

'He was that. Margaret . . . '

For the first time he appeared ill at ease.

'Is there something on your mind, Joshua?'

He crossed back to her. 'Do you remember seven or eight years ago, when Charles came to visit me in Galveston?' he asked.

'Of course. We'd endured two pitiless

years here, lost over seventy percent of our herd to the cold. I begged him not to leave, but he insisted on seeing his brother. He never could get used to your . . . disappearances.'

'He came because of you,' he said softly.

'What?'

'I was doing well at the time — very well, in fact,' he went on. 'And because he couldn't bear to see the defeat in your eyes, we struck a deal. He needed to keep this ranch . . . and insisted I hold this until he paid off the note.'

He reached into his jacket pocket and held out a folded document. She looked at it for a long moment before finally taking it, unfolding it, seeing that it was indeed what the blue backing suggested it was, and what she had feared it would be — a deed.

'This . . . ' Her voice deserted her momentarily. 'This . . . can't be.'

'You still own Carter Ranch, Margaret,' he assured her. 'It's just that now you have a . . . partner.' Seeing her look he added, 'Now, before you say anything, just think about it for a moment, about what it *means*. I can take a load off you. And Ned can learn a lot from me. You said yourself he was in search of a father figure.'

'No,' she answered. 'It was *you* who said that.' Her eyes returned again to the deed. The paper shook very slightly in her hand. 'It can't be,' she said again, still stunned by the turn their conversation had taken. 'Charles wouldn't have — '

But almost before she knew it he was so close to her that she could smell his cologne.

'Margaret,' he said earnestly, 'give this a chance. You and I together could make Carter Ranch the biggest spread in Montana.' He put his hands on her shoulders, a move that was as unexpected as it was intimate. 'Why, you and I — '

She took an instinctive step away from him. 'Leave!' she hissed.

He took another pace toward her,

reached for her again. 'Think of what you and I can build *together* . . . '

'Take your hands off me and leave!' she snapped.

For a moment he thought she might slap him. She didn't. But the revulsion he saw in her eyes as she glared at him stung even more.

'Just as you say,' he replied stiffly, and plucked the deed from between her fingers. 'But this is more than paper, Margaret. It's recorded in Galveston, and whether you like it or not, it makes me half-owner of Carter Ranch.'

He picked up his top hat and moved to the door, where he suddenly turned back. 'You'll come around,' he predicted. 'And if you don't . . . well, no matter. My mind is set, Margaret. I *will* take what is mine. And I *will* have what goes with it!'

*   *   *

The moment the door opened, Nubbs retreated back into the shadows at the top of the stairs and held his breath. After dinner he'd gone to his attic room, where he'd been painting a small wooden swan he'd carved for Kate. Though unsettled by the arrival of Joshua Carter, he'd been happy in his work. Kate would love the swan: he knew she would.

But then he'd become aware of voices downstairs — *raised* voices. And fretting for Maggie's safety, he'd left his room and cat-footed halfway down the stairs until he could hear the argument taking place in the study more clearly.

He felt bad for eavesdropping. It went against his grain. But he owed it to Charlie Carter to watch out for his wife and kids. Besides which, he'd taken an instant dislike to Joshua. Him and Charlie might be brothers, but he'd known instinctively that they were as different as night and day.

He could hear them better now.

You still own Carter Ranch, Margaret.

It's just that now you have a . . . partner.

It can't be. Charles wouldn't have —

Margaret, give this a chance. You and I together could make Carter Ranch the biggest spread in Montana. Why, you and I —

Leave!

Think of what you and I can build together . . .

Take your hands off me and leave!

Nubbs figured he'd heard enough. Jaw tightening, mind racing, hating to do what he knew he had to do, to go down there and throw Joshua out, he took another step downstairs.

Then —

Just as you say. It was Joshua, backing down. But this is more than paper. It's recorded in Galveston, and whether you like it or not, it makes me half-owner of Carter Ranch. You'll come around. And if you don't . . . well, no matter. My mind is set, Margaret. I will take what is mine. And I will have what goes with it!

116

The door opened then, and that was when Nubbs shrank back, hardly daring to breathe.

Down below, Joshua headed for the door, stuffing some papers into his inside pocket as he went. Nubbs frowned. A *deed*? A deed to the C.A. Carter Ranch? He thought again about what he'd heard, turning it over in his slow, precise way. It didn't seem like there could be much denying it.

He'd been right in his judgment of Joshua Carter, then. The man was here to make trouble for Maggie, at just the time when she could least handle it.

He listened to the sounds Joshua made outside, climbing onto his buckboard, slapping the horse to motion, turning the vehicle around and out of the yard.

You'll come around, he'd said. *And if you don't . . . well, no matter. My mind is set, Margaret. I will take what is mine. And I will have what goes with it!*

That was a threat, pure and simple.

And no one was going to threaten the Carters, not while Nubbs was around.

Something seemed to stir deep inside him then. A weird, seeping chill entered his bones, snuck into his belly. Unconsciously his right hand went to his throat, felt the rope-scars there, and when he turned and went back up to his attic room he moved like a man in a trance. There he quickly checked the time by the cheap tin clock he kept on a rough-and-ready table beside his bed. Then he shrugged into his crackly oilskin duster and clapped his old Tucson hat down firm over his scraggly hair.

He could hardly believe he was actually going to do what he'd decided to do, but he knew that to *not* do it would be to make Maggie's life a whole lot more difficult than it already was.

But to *kill* a man . . .

He thought about the Whitworth

rifle and the scope as long as its barrel that sat in the rack behind the parlor door. How many enemy soldiers had he killed with that weapon? It shamed him that he could no longer remember. Was that the worth of a man's life, then? That it could be forgotten once he'd taken it?

If that was the case, then one more life, he decided, shouldn't make a whole lot of difference. But it didn't help.

He tried to remember the last time he'd used the rifle and couldn't recall that, either, it had been so long. He'd always promised himself he'd never use it again, if he could help it.

For a moment then he was torn, remembering all the times he'd killed from concealment and over long distances. He'd always hated it, but it was war, and in war your job was to kill the other man before he killed you.

But the war was over now, had been over these past thirty years. And since that terrible day at Cold Harbor in the

119

June of '64, he'd never raised a hand in anger to another living soul.

He shook his head irritably, frustrated by his own reluctance to take up arms again.

There *must* be another way to handle this . . .

He checked the clock again, and this time noticed the half-empty bottle of whiskey standing beside it. An idea suggested itself. Quickly then, he picked up the bottle and shoved it into one of his duster's deep pockets. Then he went back to the door, opened it a crack, listened until he heard Kate return from the barn and go to her own room.

He ghosted back downstairs, keeping a careful eye on the parlor door all the while.

An eternity later the house fell behind him and the barn loomed up ahead. He made short work of saddling his Morgan horse, the coldness still in him, as was that same thought — that Joshua had threatened Maggie.

No one was going to get away with that while Nubbs was around . . . even if it meant cold-blooded murder.

7

Darkness and near-silence had settled over the Green Mountain Reservation. In the agency building, a squat, oblong cabin built from mud-chinked logs, three men sat around the table that occupied the center of the Indian Agent's quarters, a smeared bottle of rotgut whiskey between them. The mood, however, was anything but cordial.

Caleb Bateman looked from one of his companions to the other. The tiny, cluttered cabin seemed airless and confining, and the smoky lamplight did little to help. All it did was throw their shadows large up onto the supply-stocked shelves behind them.

At last Bateman said quietly, 'If you turn tail and quit now, we'll have wasted the better part of a year.'

'I wouldn't go that far,' replied

Frederick Lydecker. Lydecker, tall, cadaverous, about forty years old, had run the reservation for the past eight years. Now he tugged nervously at his blond cow-horn mustache. 'You've turned a handsome profit from it, Bateman, and you know it. The minute them cows crossed onto the reservation there wasn't hide nor hair that could be traced back to you. My Sioux got fed and you walked away with top dollar.'

Bateman curled his lip at that. 'Ten, fifteen head at a time ain't hardly worth the trouble,' he said, 'and you can be damn' sure it ain't worth the risk. My men're lookin' for a payday, Fred, and they sure don't figure to endure another winter at that damned relay station no one uses anymore.'

Lydecker's strained tone matched his expression, and above his waxed-paper collar his Adam's apple twitched. 'I'm telling you, we need to quit while we can.'

Bateman held his stare for a long,

heavy moment. He could be warm and friendly when it suited him. When it didn't, he became something much different, something harder, more spiteful, a man whom you could believe had killed before and would be happy enough to kill again, if there was profit or personal satisfaction to be gained from it.

Without warning his eyes shuttled to the third man, and he said, 'Ned?'

Ned Carter glanced across at Lydecker and weighed his response. Hesitantly he said, 'Accordin' to my ma, Sheriff McKenna's still snoopin' around.'

'He's *always* snoopin',' said Bateman dismissively. 'It's what lawmen *do.*'

'Sure. But that's not all. Cyrus McCall's started talkin' about doin' some snoopin' of his own — and dispensin' a little hemp justice when he tracks us down.'

Bateman fell silent as he pondered that. At length he said, 'Don't include yourself in this, boy.'

'Don't call me that.'

Bateman nodded. 'All right. But I mean it, Ned. You're my friend, and you've been a help, but don't you go throwing in with us, not if it's the way you say. You've shown us the trails we've used to run them cattle all the way here, you set us up in that abandoned stagecoach station along Creek Run, and I'm beholden. But I guess it was only a matter of time until it came to this, and that's why I always tried to keep you out of it.'

'You don't have to go protectin' me,' said Ned. 'I can look after myself.'

'Not at the end of a hangrope you can't. No man can. And only a fool courts the rope when he don't have to.'

'Well,' Ned sighed, 'Fred's got a point, I reckon. Things are gettin' too risky. Besides, there's somethin' else I picked up from my girl.'

Bateman's beard stirred a little with his smile. 'That Georgia Lamb? Mighty fine-looking woman, Ned. You're a lucky man.'

'She said she heard that Cyrus's now got men in the saddle all of the day and most of the night. It's only a matter of time before you ride right into them. And then you might not live long enough for the rope, 'cause it'll come to shootin', right there, right then.'

'He's right, Cal,' Lydecker said, hoping to press the point home. 'Best we all quit now, while the quitting's good.'

Temper slipping, Bateman suddenly slammed a palm down on the table. The sound it made seemed thunderous, and the bottle and glasses clinked discordantly.

'I'll tell you when you're out!' he snarled. 'Now listen good, Lydecker. I aim to drive a hundred and fifty head of Cyrus McCall's cattle to the reservation tomorrow night. I'm comin' right through McCall's fence and across your land, Ned, same as always.' His eyes seemed to drill into the Indian Agent. 'An' there better be three thousand dollars waiting for me when I get here,

Fred. So long as there is, you'll never lay eyes on me again.'

He didn't have to spell out the alternative. Lydecker's imagination did that for him.

'That's crazy,' Lydecker whispered. 'Where would I get three thousand dollars?'

'Well, don't tell me you ain't already got it! The Government grants you the right to pay up to fifty dollars a head for cattle to feed these here tame Sioux o' yours! You pay me half that an' pocket the rest! Now, you have that money ready, Fred. Come hell or high water, them cows are coming in tomorrow night . . . and I won't take kindly to any disappointment.'

★ ★ ★

On the trail back to Singletree, Joshua Carter swore irritably. He'd known there would be resistance, of course. You didn't just walk in on someone's life after eight long years and expect them to let you take over. But he'd been sure that, by appealing to Maggie's sensibilities, by reminding her of just how vulnerable she was out here, just what it would mean for the ranch to have a man around the place again to guide it to the greatness she so desired, he might be able to change her mind.

He had a glib tongue, he knew that. He'd charmed women all the way from Yucatàn to Cuba and never failed to get his way with them. But what he'd seen in Maggie's eyes tonight had startled him. It had been a mixture of hate and disgust and absolute determination to fight him for his half-ownership in the C.A. Carter every step of the way.

Oh, he had no doubt that he'd win, eventually. He had the law on his side. But sometimes the law could drag its heels. There was always the chance the judge might look a little more sympathetically on a woman — a *widow* — than a man. And he had always considered Maggie to be a handsome woman. Indeed, it was his hope to inherit his brother's wife as well as his ranch.

But now it looked as if he was in for a fight of it, and knowing that he cursed softly but with feeling under his breath.

Transferring the reins to one hand, he reached into his jacket pocket and drew out a cigar. He thrust the fine *La Flor de Cano* into his mouth, searched for a match and cursed again. Where were his matches?

With little thought for the horse, he yanked back on the reins, bringing the buckboard to a halt, then wound the reins around the brake handle and hopped down onto the trail. The night — considerably cooler now — was lit by a sickle moon, the contours of the trail, the surrounding hills, the cauliflower tops of trees, limned in cold silver. He reached into the back of the wagon for his carpetbag, opened it and rummaged for matches.

After a few seconds he found

them, extracted one, struck it against the side of the buckboard and made to light his cigar. A stray breeze blew up and stole the flame away. Shaking his head, Joshua took out a second match —

And that was when he heard it.

Something out in the darkness, creeping closer.

The horse heard it as well, and spooked, leaned forward into the harness. The brake-locked wheels dragged a little through the dirt and Joshua panicked, called nervously, 'Wh-whoa!'

The horse stopped, but continued to eye its surroundings with head high, hooves stamping restively.

'Who's out there?' Joshua called.

There was no answer.

Quickly he fumbled in an inside pocket, brought out the nickel-plated Colt Cloverleaf he was seldom without. Staring out into the darkness he called, 'I'm armed! Y-you'd better identify yourself!'

A breeze blew up, then died. Joshua

strained his ears. The night suddenly fell still, silent. He thought about mountain lions. He'd heard they roamed the high country hereabouts. Maybe one had wandered down to a lower elevation in search of food. If so, he seriously doubted that a .41-caliber bullet would do much to stop it.

'I — ' he began, and then he heard something away to his right.

He twisted, cried out when he saw the silhouette of a big, hulking man no more than a dozen feet away, then jabbed the Cloverleaf out ahead of him and pulled the trigger. The gun spat flame and his target quickly dodged to one side and then came at him in a run.

Joshua cried out again, but before he could fire the pocket pistol a second time his assailant was on him, his weight shoving Joshua back hard against the side of the buckboard.

For a moment they grappled, and the night filled with the sounds they made struggling. Joshua felt the other man close fingers around his throat and as his air was blocked off he panicked still more, tightened his palm around the Colt's pearl grips, stabbed it into the larger man's belly and pulled the trigger again.

The shot was muffled by his attacker's duster, but even so Joshua felt him jerk, buckle, stumble back, and knew a sudden thrill of excitement. He'd killed the man! The devil had tried to attack him and rob him and instead all he'd collected for his trouble was a bullet!

He straightened up, sucking air greedily, consumed by the urge to put another bullet in the bastard and look into his eyes as he died knowing he'd picked on the wrong —

Then the hulking figure, hatless now, straightened back to his full height, and as he did so the moonlight showed his face for the first time and —

Joshua went cold.

It was Margaret's hired man . . . Nubbins!

He thought he understood it all, then.

That *bitch!* She'd sent this brute out to steal the deed from him or, God forbid, *kill* him!

Filled with anger now, he fired the weapon's final two shots, and each muzzle flash showed Nubbs' face as he came closer, closer —

Then Nubbs backhanded Joshua with every ounce of strength he had in him. Joshua's head snapped sideways and he crumpled, unconscious, the gun slipping from his fingers.

Nubbs stood over him, broad shoulders rising and falling as he gasped for air. He'd been hit, and the world was spinning around him. He stepped over the unconscious man and leaned against the buckboard for a moment, until the spinning slowed. Then he turned toward the moonlight, unbuttoned the blood-slick duster and inspected the wound as best he could.

He grimaced. He'd been shot high on the left side of his chest. The wound hurt bad, but when he explored it with his fingertips he realized that one of his ribs, now chipped, had turned the bullet before it could penetrate and chew him up inside. He was lucky it hadn't been any worse.

He didn't feel especially lucky right then, though. He looked down at Joshua and felt a stab of dread. Even if he'd been of a mind to do so, there could be no backing out now. He was committed to seeing this thing through.

Suddenly he remembered the whiskey bottle in his pocket, brought it out, took a jolt. He closed his eyes, clenched his teeth and waited for the pain to pass, then fumbled out a kerchief and used it to plug the wound. He would live, he knew that. But it would take time to heal, and if he returned to the ranch, he'd have to explain how he'd come by his wound. Besides, when word of Joshua's fate got back to Maggie, he was by no means sure he'd be able to look her in the eye if she put two and two together.

In the distance he heard a low, somber whistle of the eight-forty to Fort Clark. It sharpened his senses a little, reminded him that there was no time to lose now, not if he wanted to do this right.

He scooped up Joshua's Colt Cloverleaf. He'd throw it in the creek first chance he got. Then he lifted the unconscious man and threw him into the buckboard. Joshua bounced a little against the long, springy boards. Then Nubbs quickly searched the unconscious man's pockets until he found the deed. This he crammed into one of his own pockets.

He disappeared back into the trees then, stumbling a little now, and favoring his left side more noticeably. A short time later he reemerged with his own Morgan, which he tethered to the buckboard's thin iron tie rail.

Beginning to feel a little feverish, he hauled himself up into the buckboard's seat. The flimsy vehicle tilted beneath him. He took the reins, kicked off the brake and turned the vehicle around. He had to reach the railroad tracks ahead of the eight-forty to Fort Clark.

8

The next morning Maggie woke with purpose, skipped breakfast, saddled Sundown and left the yard without a backward glance.

She held the pace more or less all the way into Singletree. She was in a foul mood and nothing was going to stop her from clawing back control of her life.

The best she'd managed the previous night was a fitful half-doze that was filled with nightmares. The sudden appearance of Charles's brother and his claim of half-ownership in the ranch had been the last thing she'd expected, and it made her despair in a way she had never previously thought possible. What else had to happen? What else did she have to endure before everything came right for her?

After a while she'd given up trying to

sleep at all. Instead she'd flopped into her chair by the window and watched the stars in their courses, and tried to organize her jumbled thoughts. Joshua was nobody's fool. If he said the deed was legal, she could be sure it was. He knew she would fight his claim to half-ownership in the Charles A. Carter Ranch, knew his papers would come under expert scrutiny, and would take no chances with forgeries, no matter how clever they might be.

But for the time being, Joshua would have to wait. For now, she had another concern — Ned.

He'd left the ranch after supper last night and had not returned with the dawn. There was only one place he could be, and she decided that this . . . this infatuation Ned had with Georgia Lamb had gone far enough. She was damned if she'd see him squander the chance she and Charles had worked so hard to give him, and damned indeed if she would risk the future of the ranch to the whims of a glorified saloon girl.

She drew rein outside the saloon, swung down and shoved through the batwings. Sam Larch, Georgia's barkeeper, was restocking the shelves and saw her stride past in the back bar mirror. He turned, called, 'Hey! Mrs. Carter? Mrs. Carter, you can't go up there!'

But he was too late. Maggie was already climbing the stairs beside the tiny stage, her feet setting up an insistent echo that shattered the peace.

She reached the gallery, strode down the hallway, thinking that this was where Ned wasted his time, in the arms of that . . . that . . .

But she didn't want to think about that. Ned was her boy. She didn't want to think of him as anything else. She reached the door at the end of the hallway and thumped at it with one small, clenched fist.

A few moments later the door opened a crack and Georgia's face appeared, wearing a frown that slackened off when she recognized Maggie. Before she could say anything, Maggie demanded, 'I've come for my son.'

'Ned's not here,' Georgia replied. 'I haven't seen him in two days.'

Maggie didn't believe her. Seeing as much in her face, the way her eyes immediately focused on the room behind her, Georgia swung the door wide. 'Check under the bed, if you like,' she said without humor.

Maggie looked at the room. It was neat and tidy, a woman's room. More than that, it was the room of a woman of refinement, not at all the dingy, unswept crib of a prostitute.

'Mrs. Carter,' said Georgia, 'can I ask you something?'

'I suppose,' Maggie said grudgingly.

'Ned is a man full-grown. Why can't you accept that?'

'I *do* accept it,' Maggie replied. 'But that doesn't mean I have to stand by and watch while he sullies himself in a . . . a cesspool like *this*.'

Georgia's eyes widened at the same

time her jaw firmed up. 'At least I make him feel like a man, and not a little boy who needs punishing!'

For Maggie that was the last straw. Without pausing to consider the consequences, she allowed her normal, iron control to slip and slapped Georgia across the face. Georgia's head twisted sideways, her skin turning pale beneath her rouge. For one split instant she was too startled to realize even what had just happened, much less react to it.

But then she *did* react.

As she came back around she threw a punch — not a slap — right at Maggie's jaw.

The pain was tremendous, and as Maggie stumbled backwards it blotted out everything else. She thought, *I've been punched. She punched me!* And then her temper flared white-hot and she straightened, tasting blood on her teeth, and threw herself at the other woman with fingers clawed.

They collided and Maggie's greater weight threw Georgia back into the room. The backs of Georgia's knees connected with the edge of the bed and she went down on the coverlet with Maggie on top of her, her face all eyes and lips drawn back in a snarl.

Maggie grabbed her around the throat. Beneath her, Georgia squirmed like an eel. She lashed out, caught Maggie a glancing blow that tumbled her hat from her head and set her red-auburn locks spilling around her face.

Almost before she realized it, her hands found Georgia's exposed throat, tightened around it and kept tightening . . .

Maggie looked down at her, aware of nothing but the rage she had for so long kept contained within her: that, and Georgia's eyes. They were all she could see now, those green eyes, open wide, showing fear, *real* fear that Maggie would not stop until she had throttled every last drop of life from her wriggling body.

Then someone came up behind Maggie — Sam Larch. He grabbed her by the arms and hauled her back off his employer. Maggie fought him every inch of the way, arms and legs flailing.

'Ma'am . . . Mrs. Carter . . . '

But she was crazy now, her fighting blood up. Sam saw it in the way she looked at him when finally she dragged herself from his grip and twisted around to glare up at him, and much as it grieved him to do so, he did the only thing he could.

He slapped her, hard.

Maggie rocked back on her heels, came partway back from whatever dark place she'd been to, realized he'd hit her and her lips curled back off her teeth. Sam braced himself for her response, but almost in the same moment she realized *why* he'd slapped her, and something seemed to drain out of her. She sagged. The fire left her eyes. And in that moment she looked completely baffled, and mortified that she had lowered herself to such a level.

She glanced across at Georgia, sitting up now, eyes watering, one hand exploring the bruised flesh of her throat. She couldn't stand what she saw in Georgia's expression and quickly turned, snatched up her hat and left.

* * *

She was hardly aware of the ride home. All she could think about was the way everything in her life was slipping away from her.

Was this some kind of divine judgment? Had she become so warped by the life she'd led that God felt the need to punish her? She couldn't really believe that. There were a lot of evil people in this world, and she knew she wasn't one of them. It couldn't be evil to want the best for your children, to have built a wonderful ranch and to want to make it bigger and better still.

Then she remembered the Navy Colt in the chest in her room. She had fired that gun once before, though more in fear than anger. Still, she had fired it in defense of her very life, when she was still young and had decided that she wasn't going to let her stepfather rape her ever again.

The shot had been intended to warn him off. Instead it had hit him a glancing blow in the fleshy part of his left arm. He'd staggered and cried out. In what little moonlight filled her room, she'd seen the bright spray of blood and convinced herself that she'd killed him.

She hadn't, of course. She couldn't have lived with that knowledge — then. But she had wounded him, and knowing what a vile, intemperate man he was, she had taken her mother's advice and fled.

Sometimes she felt she'd been fleeing ever since.

But could that have been the reason for what seemed like an endless procession of ill fortune? Because she had *almost* killed a man?

Abruptly she was tired of trying to understand the crooked trail her life had taken. Besides, she needed a clear head if she were to deal with Joshua's claim to half-ownership of the ranch.

She rode into the yard, handed Sundown over to the first hired hand she saw and let herself into the house. Not in any mood for company right then, and certainly unwilling to let anyone see the marks of the fight she still bore, she climbed the stairs to her room and quietly, almost wearily, let herself inside.

She went directly to the dresser, bent and studied her face in the mirror. She looked rumpled and flustered, but incredibly there were no bruises or scratches. That was something —

Her eyes strayed from her reflection then, and she saw it sitting in the center of her desk — Nubbs' small, beaded possibles bag.

Slowly she took off her hat and hung it on a peg in the back of the door. She had no idea what the bag signified, but she had an uncanny conviction that it could mean nothing good.

Had something happened to Nubbs? He'd been with them so long that she wasn't sure if she could take that, on top of everything else.

She went around the desk and picked the bag up almost reluctantly. She peeled back the decorated flap, reached inside, brought out —

It was a small, exquisitely carved, partially painted swan.

For me? she wondered. No. This would be for Kate — the apple of his eye.

Then why had he left it with Maggie?

She reached into the bag again and as her fingers closed around something that felt very much like some kind of folded document, she thought she knew.

No. No, Nubbs, no . . .

She took out the document, knew at once that it was the deed that gave Joshua his half-share in the ranch, and thought she knew how he must have obtained it. But . . .

No, not Nubbs. Nubbs wouldn't hurt a fly.

Unless . . .

Unless that fly was set on hurting the Carters.

The deed trembled in her fingers, until at last she let it drop to the desk, beside the swan. Then she hurried from the room, up the stairs to Nubbs' attic quarters, opened the door —

Empty.

He was gone.

Gone . . .

In a panic now, she went downstairs, asked Hester if she'd seen Nubbs today. She hadn't. Outside she asked after him among the men. No one had seen him. In the barn she checked the stall where he always quartered his Morgan. The stall was empty.

She stood there, fists clenched at her sides, shivering, guessing what had happened, what Nubbs had chosen to do about it. And the consequences.

Oh, Nubbs . . .

'Mother?'

Startled, she turned guiltily, saw Kate silhouetted in the barn doorway. Clearing her throat she said, 'What, ah . . . what is it, Kathryn?'

'The marshal's here,' Kate replied.

'He wants to see you.'

Nubbs . . .

She struggled to bring her nerves under control, squared her shoulders and said, 'Tell him I'll, ah . . . be out directly.'

Kate hesitated. 'Are you all right, Mother?'

'Of course I am.'

Kate nodded, not looking at all convinced, then turned and left her there.

She held back a moment longer, trying to compose herself, then finally strode as confidently as she could out into the sunlight. McKenna was standing beside his horse before the house, Kate next to him. He watched her come with an expression he couldn't decipher.

She didn't want to risk speaking. Her voice might betray her. But she knew she had to say something. Somehow she managed, 'Kathryn — leave us, would you?'

Kate did so. When she was gone

Maggie said, 'I think I can guess why you're here, Matthew. It's . . . Georgia Lamb, isn't it? She wants to press charges against me for a . . . uh . . . disagreement we had earlier.'

McKenna definitely looked ill at ease — she wasn't just imagining it. 'I heard about that,' he replied uncomfortably. 'Word about a thing like that has a habit of spreading, Mrs. Carter. But no: far as I'm aware, Georgia's got no plans to press charges.'

'Then — '

'Do you happen to know a man by the name of Joshua Carter?' he asked suddenly.

'Yes. He's my brother-in-law.'

'When did you last see him, ma'am?'

'Last night. He showed up unexpectedly. He'd been . . . overseas, I believe and . . . and only just heard about Charles's death. He shared a meal with us, we . . . we spoke of Charles for a while . . . ' Forcing herself to take the bull by the horns, she said, 'Sheriff . . . why are you asking after Joshua?'

She braced herself. *Here it comes,* she thought. *He's going to tell me that Joshua has been robbed and injured, and that he's identified Nubbs as his assailant.*

'He's dead, Mrs. Carter,' said the sheriff.

She swayed visibly. *'Wh-what?'*

'Near as we can figure, he lost his way back to town. Team led him down to railroad tracks that run through Oak Hollow. Seems he took a tumble, hit his head and lost consciousness . . . on the tracks.'

'No!' She didn't have to pretend horror at what he was telling her.

'He was still there when the eight-forty went through. Engineer didn't even know he'd hit him.'

She looked down at her feet, wondering if that was really the way of it, that Nubbs, out for some reason, had simply taken advantage of the situation —

But no.

'Mrs. Carter?'

'Uh . . . I'm sorry, Matthew. What did you say?'

'I asked if the deceased had anything to drink when he was here last night?'

'Yes. Wine. An after-dinner brandy.'

'That all?'

'What do you mean?'

'I don't like to speak ill of the dead, but Mr. Carter smelled strongly of whiskey when we found him, and there was the remnants of a pint bottle of whiskey on his person. My guess is that he drank while he was here and all but finished off a bottle of whiskey on his way back to town. That's how he came to leave the trail without realizing it, and why he fell off his buckboard.'

'Th-that certainly makes sense,' she said carefully. Then, almost to herself: 'A stupid, tragic accident.'

At least that's the way Nubbs made it look.

'Yes'm. I'm sorry to've brought you the news.'

'That . . . that's all right, Sheriff. If you would be so kind as to arrange burial in the town cemetery, I w-will of course pay for the funeral.'

'I will, Mrs. Carter. Thank you.'

'It's nothing,' she replied, and then added: 'It's the least I can do.'

9

Darkness had fallen like a velvet cape across the McCall spread, and a cool breeze sent clouds scudding north across the sky to obscure the moon.

It was a good night for rustling.

Caleb Bateman smiled at the thought. Of course, as far as he was concerned, *any* night was a good night for rustling, provided a man did his job and didn't get caught. But he'd meant what he'd told Lydecker the night before. The risks were the same whether you set out to lift ten head or ten times that number. Only the reward differed. And there wasn't much reward to be had from lifting a dozen head here and fifteen there.

He'd meant something else he'd said, too. His men *were* getting restless, cooped up as they were down at the old abandoned way station on Creek Run. A couple of them had already started making barely-veiled comments about Bateman's abilities to lead them. It was the kind of talk he had to nip in the bud, and as with most things in life, it was actions that spoke louder than words.

So he'd announced his intention to lift a hundred and fifty head in one go, to run them up to the reservation and make some real money. Then he and his boys would clear the county and set up someplace new. He liked the sound of Texas about now . . .

The soft jingle of bit and harness drew him from his reverie. He hipped around as Frank Shelley rode up. In the darkness behind him Bateman heard the familiar sounds of cattle on the move.

'All clear, Cal?' Shelley asked softly.

Bateman's teeth showed in a brief grin. 'As glass,' he replied. He backed away from the wire he'd just cut and said, 'Run 'em through.'

* * *

Rachel McCall had always been an excellent cook, but tonight she'd provided a veritable feast that included a starter of caramelized onion tart, followed by dove casserole, hashed potatoes and collard greens, with buttermilk pie for dessert. When Cyrus McCall had asked her what the occasion was, the pretty, dark-haired half-breed, who was ten years her husband's junior, had looked at him as if the answer should be obvious.

'We have company,' she said, and looking across the table at their guest, Simon Doubleday, rolled her dark hazel eyes.

'Company?' Cyrus repeated with a scowl. 'Newspapermen ain't company. They're a damn' nuisance.'

'Pay him no mind, Simon. You're always welcome here, and you know it.'

'Indeed I do, Rachel,' the reporter replied. Doubleday was in his early forties, with prematurely gray hair swept back off a patrician face and a military mustache of the same color. He smiled as he added pointedly, 'At least *you* have manners.'

'Better watch what you say at my table,' growled Cyrus.

'I am merely offering the truth.'

Rachel served Simon first, leaving Cyrus clearly miffed. 'The truth? Think a newspaperman'd be likely to recognize that, was he to see it?'

'You're an unkind man, Cyrus McCall. I've never lied in my life.'

'An' water ain't wet, I suppose?'

Rachel sighed. 'Will you two behave?'

But it was too late: Simon had already sensed an opening. 'Speaking of water,' he said carefully, 'what do you intend to do about Maggie Carter, Cyrus? As I understand it, her cows *do* have to walk a far piece for water since you strung your wire.'

Cyrus's well-weathered face darkened, for he was a rancher born and the stringing of barbed wire had given him no pleasure. 'I don't like fences anymore'n the next man. But when we start losin' twenty, thirty head a month, somethin's got to be done. 'Sides, it was nothin' personal. We all know they was crossin' Carter land.'

'I know that well enough. I've written about Big Sky losses a dozen times, remember. It's just that fences . . . they rub people the wrong way, Cyrus.'

'You mean my fences rub Maggie *Carter* the wrong way.'

'Mostly. But she's — '

'But nothin', Simon. Listen — I ain't sayin' Maggie's got any hand in this, but the fact is, I was losin' cows, an' somethin' had to be done, even if it was somethin' nobody much cared for. Now, you an' me, we've put up with each other ever since you came to Singletree, so let's not spoil five years of mutual tolerance by extendin' this here conversation any further. In other words — mind your own business.'

'That's the trouble, Cyrus,' Doubleday persisted. 'Other peoples' business *is* my business.'

Cyrus fixed the newspaperman with a glare, his eyes turning decidedly chilly. 'Then there's one thing you better get straight,' he growled softly. '*My* business ain't *yours*. You got it?'

That had always been Cyrus's way. And for her part, Rachel shared his feelings toward Maggie Carter. It hadn't always been that way, though. The fact that she'd threatened Cyrus over the fence made her something of an enemy, but Rachel couldn't help but respect her courage, and secretly she envied her because she had a beautiful daughter.

The McCalls had been married for thirty-five years. Rachel's father had been a scout for the army, her mother a full-blooded Sioux. She was as resilient as her husband — as a half-breed she'd had to be — but though she seemed to live her life with good humor, outwardly at least, one thing had always played on her mind. She had only ever been able to bring one of her many pregnancies to full term.

Val had carried without a problem and was nothing short of perfect at birth, but she had always been haunted by the feeling that she had somehow let Cyrus down by not bearing more children.

It was a notion Cyrus himself had always dismissed, claiming that Val did the work of three sons, anyway. And if they'd had any girls, he would continue, well, the thought of having yet more women in the house to boss him around still brought the hairs up on his neck.

For a moment a heavy silence descended over the dining table, and finally taking the hint, Simon Doubleday changed the subject to something slightly less contentious — namely, the chances of Cyrus deciding to run for mayor in the upcoming elections.

'All I'm saying,' said Simon, 'is that Wes Rickey just isn't up to the job. Sure, he's got influence with the miners, but . . . well, I'll say it plain. He doesn't command authority. Face it, Cyrus — *you're* the man for the job. People listen when you talk.'

'He's right,' said Rachel.

'No way in hell,' was Cyrus's terse response. 'Besides, I never been much for words.' He sent a meaningful glower in Simon's direction. 'For some, they come too damn' easy.'

The newspaperman let that slide. 'It's your civic duty,' he argued.

'Simon Double-Damned Doubleday, there ain't enough money in — '

Before he could finish, the parlor door burst open and Val stamped inside with a face like thunder. 'Sorry to interrupt,' he said, 'but we got trouble, Pa.'

McCall pushed up out of his chair, the earlier conversation instantly forgotten. 'Them rustlers again?'

Val nodded. 'Down along Wildcat Draw. The fence's been cut. Looks like the sonsa — ' He broke off, threw an apologetic glance at his mother. 'Looks like they've taken seventy, eighty head this time.'

'Wildcat Draw?'

'Yeah. It was Billy Broken Hand who

spotted the cut wire. He says if they're takin' 'em north through Wildcat Draw, they could easily push 'em in a wide circle and then come up on the Green Mountain Reservation from the east.'

Doubleday also rose, sensing a story. 'Is Billy saying it's the Indian Agent, what's his name — Lydecker — who's been rustling the stock all this time?'

'He's sayin' it's the nearest place anyone could run 'em to and have 'em butchered and eaten before anyone knows they're missin'.'

'Well, we won't go makin' any wild accusations till we know for sure,' Cyrus said in his customary rumble. 'But it sure looks like we got 'em this time.' He fixed his son with a stern eye. 'Rouse the men. Them sons can't have gone far, an' they'll be leavin' plenty sign behind 'em, pushin' that many cows. We should be able to catch up in next to no time.'

'Cyrus . . . ' began Rachel.

Glancing at her, Cyrus jabbed a finger at his son. 'An' you stay here with your mother.' Though he didn't say it, Val read the rest of the sentence in his tone.

Just in case.

'Ain't likely, Pa,' Val replied.

Cyrus saw that there was no way he would talk his son out of the decision he'd already made. And when it came down to it, Val had as much of a right to protect McCall stock as he did himself. He could hardly deny the boy that.

'Then go saddle my horse,' he said, 'an' we'll ride together.'

Val nodded, paused just long enough to kiss his mother and then left the room.

Rachel stared up at her husband, who now did everything he could to avoid her gaze. 'You should leave this to Matt McKenna,' she said.

'Ain't got time for that,' McCall replied, taking a coiled gun belt from a bureau drawer and hoping he hadn't outgrown it. 'Time he gets here, they'll be long gone.'

'Then lend me a gun and a

saddle-horse and let me go with you,' said Simon.

'The hell with *that.*'

'I'm a newspaperman, Cyrus! I can't miss this story!'

'And I can't spare the time to nurse a greenhorn!'

'You don't have to worry about me! I'll take my chances!'

There was no time to argue about it. McCall said shortly, 'All right. Help yourself to one of the Winchesters in yonder rack. There's shells in the top drawer. And while you're at it, I'll tell you this. It ain't gonna be pretty, what happens out there tonight. If you live to see tomorrow's sunrise, you'll be a changed man.'

★ ★ ★

It was all going according to plan: so much so that Bateman could already feel that three thousand dollars in his pocket. 'Course, he knew the risk he was running. You couldn't push this

164

many cows and not leave a trail behind you that even a blind man could follow. But this time out, that was no concern of his. By the time McCall's men discovered the loss and went for the sheriff, him and the rest of his boys would be a good long ways from here. Then it would be Lydecker's problem, and he'd have the devil's own time explaining why the trail led straight to Green Mountain.

The thought of that mealy-mouthed Indian Agent squirming only added to his pleasure.

'What's so funny?' asked Ned, beside him. His voice was tight, nervous. 'Damned if I can see anything to laugh about right now.'

'Relax,' said Bateman. 'Relax and hold your nerve. It was you who insisted on comin' along, remember? I'd have been happier to see you well out of it.'

''Cause I'm just a kid?' Ned asked sullenly. 'I'm a man full-grown.'

'You're that, all right,' Bateman returned. They rode on for a few yards, the other men continuing to push the cattle along behind them. Then Ned said, 'You mean that, Cal?'

'Mean what?'

'What you said just now?'

'About you bein' a man?'

'Uh-huh.'

'Wouldn't have said it if I didn't mean it.'

There was another lengthy pause, until Ned said, 'Means a lot to me. Comin' from you, I mean. You've known plenty men in your time, I reckon, and bark on all of 'em.'

'Well, you could ride with the best, Ned Carter. You take that from me.'

'When do you, ah . . . figure on quittin' the territory?'

'Soon as we get our money from Lydecker. Sun-up, maybe. A little after.'

'I'd appreciate to ride with you, when you go.'

That surprised Bateman. He couldn't figure why anyone would want to turn his back on the C.A. Carter Ranch. But then he thought about Maggie

Carter, and all the stories Ned had told him about her, and then he sort of understood.

'This isn't the life for you, Ned,' he answered presently, choosing his words carefully. 'Man has to be a special kind of fool to ride the owlhoot trail. You got more sense'n that.'

'Maybe I have,' said Ned. 'But I ain't got too much reason. Two women in my life — three, if you count my sister — and not one of 'em thinks I'll ever amount to anything.'

'So stay put and prove 'em wrong. You sure as hell won't prove anythin' by runnin' with the likes of us. Fact is, you'll only prove they was right all along.'

He drew rein suddenly. The palomino walked on a few paces before Ned also halted. 'What is it, Cal?'

Bateman looked him directly in the face. All each of them was to the other was a smudge of shadow paler than the rest, relieved every so often by the glisten of eye or teeth.

'I know why you threw in with us,' he

said softly, and suddenly there was something in his voice, a kind of compassion, almost, that Ned found startling. 'You were sick and tired of being a nobody — the nobody your ma said you were. And you had a powerful hate for McCall's son, 'cause of what happened to your face. You figured that ridin' with us gave you the kind of friends you couldn't get anyplace else. Bein' one of us made you somebody. And lettin' us push McCall's stock across your land helped you pay McCall's boy back some of what you owed him, an' purty much the same with your ma.

'Well, you did all those things, Ned. You *are* someone. 'Fact, you always were, you just never saw it for yourself. You *did* make pals here, with me and the boys. And we sure as shootin' made the McCalls *pay*, didn't we?

'But a *real* man — a *wise* man — he knows when to quit. That's where you and me split the blanket, Ned. You got the sense to do like Lydecker said, and get out while the gettin's good.'

'And you?'

'Too late for me and the boys, I reckon. We've already chosen our trail.'

'I won't slow you down, if that's what you're trying to say.'

'It's not. But if someone had told me just what I was lettin' myself in for before I got into this line of work, maybe things'd been different. A wife, kids, little spread of my own, maybe.'

'Maybe that's not what I want.'

Again Bateman smiled. 'That's what your mouth says,' he said. 'But I 'spect your heart says the opposite.'

By now the rustled stock was filing past them. The herd smelled of dirt and heat, grass and money. Bateman said, 'You've proved everythin' you need to prove, I reckon. Now turn that horse around and head for home.'

Ned opened his mouth to protest, but Bateman talked him down.

'It's over, Ned. You've evened the score. Go back to your old life while it's still there to go back to.'

He offered his hand.

Ned stared at it, unwilling to believe that this man he had come to idolize was just about to ride out of his life forever. For a moment he felt the way he'd felt when his father had died, and felt the quick sting of tears. But he'd be damned if he'd show them. Much as he didn't want to admit it, Caleb was right. Whatever hatreds had driven him to throw in with Bateman and his men had been quenched now. No one would ever know that he'd helped the rustlers, much less that he'd ridden with them. But *he* would know. He would know that he *had* been someone, if only for a few short months.

Besides, that talk of a wife and kids . . . it had pointed his thoughts back toward Georgia. Who needed the C.A. Carter Ranch, anyway? Better to turn his back on it, on his mother, and make a better, happier life for him and Georgia both, while he still could.

He reached out and shook with Bateman.

'I'll miss you, pard,' he said.

'Not when you're tucked up tight and warm in your girlfriend's arms you won't,' said Bateman. He was silent for a long moment, until at length he said, 'Go on, get out of here.'

'You sure — '

'We can finish up here, I reckon.'

The cows continued to file past. At last Ned gathered his reins and tugged his horse around.

'So long,' he said.

He couldn't trust himself to say anything more.

10

The trail was clear to see in the moonlight. As Cyrus McCall stood up in his stirrups to survey it, he thought, *Seventy, eighty head be damned. They're pushing a hundred of my stock at least. Likely more.*

He dropped his bulk back down into the saddle and turned to the men who had bunched up behind him.

'We got 'em,' he said. 'An' I reckon they're gonna make a fight of it, 'cause we all know what happens to cattle-thieves after they get caught. Any man here got anythin' against havin' to shoot and maybe kill another man?'

A few horses stamped restively. Bit chains jingled, leather gear squeaked. Clutching the Winchester he'd helped himself to, Simon Doubleday swallowed hard. But no man there backed down.

'All right,' said McCall. 'Take off

your hats and pack 'em away some-wheres safe.'

Doubleday frowned. 'What's that?'

'It's black as a poacher's pocket out here, Simon, an' there's gonna be shootin'. You see a man in a hat, he's the man you're after. You see a man without one, he's one of your own.'

Wordlessly the men took off their hats and shoved them inside jackets or saddlebags. Then came the metallic clicks and spins and ratchet sounds of men checking their weapons. Double-day felt cold and fearful.

'Ready?' McCall asked at last.

There was a muttered chorus of assent.

'Let's ride,' said the rancher.

★ ★ ★

Riding drag on the herd, Chester Furlong — a skinny man with a squint in his left eye — had no idea there was going to be trouble tonight. So far, everything had gone exactly to plan, and he was already thinking about just how he was going to spend his share of the take.

Then, above the shuffle, snuffle and bawl of the cattle he heard something else, and thought, *Dammit. Sounds like we got a storm comin'*.

Even as he thought it, however, the sound increased in volume, grew clearer, and at last he sat bolt upright in his saddle.

That's not thunder — that's horses, comin' fast!

In almost the same instant someone far behind him yelled, '*Stop right where you are, you sonofabitch!*'

Furlong turned in the saddle, saw the silhouettes of maybe a dozen men just coming up and over a ridge to the west and down into the swale he and the others were now pushing the stolen cattle across. Panicking, he clawed for the .45 worn high at his hip.

One of McCall's hands thrust his own gun to arm's length and fired. The shot sounded twice as loud as it should have, coming out of the darkness like it did, and more by luck than design it slammed the rustler sideways out of his saddle with a ruined left shoulder.

Already spooked at having to move at night, the stolen cattle immediately started blatting and milling in every direction.

As Cyrus McCall's riders came down into the swale, Bateman, riding point on the herd, yanked his mount around and swore. Instinctively he palmed his Colt, but he had no intention of fighting if he could help it. That these fellers were playing for keeps had already been established. He yelled, 'Scatter!' and then heeled his own horse into motion. He'd head for the way station, wait for the others to regroup there and then consider his options.

But the McCall riders had other ideas — as did the land itself. The swale, not quite marshy but moist enough to make mud, meant that a quick getaway was all but impossible. As horses slipped and slid, McCall's men came galloping in with guns blazing. The first volley was withering; it cut down men and horses both, the screams of the wounded and dying heard even above the bellowing of frightened cattle.

One rustler crashed hard to the ground and quickly threw himself out of the way before his dead horse could land on top of him. He scooped his .45 from leather, snap-aimed at the nearest rider and returned fire. Val McCall swore he felt the wind of the bullet as it flew past him and for just a moment thereafter froze solid. Then instinct kicked in, he turned to the man and fired two shots in reply. The rustler jerked, backpedaled, went down writhing.

A cow collapsed, grunting, as a stray bullet slammed her in the flank. Partway through tearing his Winchester from its scabbard, another rustler somersaulted out of his saddle, a crimson spray busting from his chest.

There was chaos everywhere as the

two opposing forces clashed. Still the rustlers tried to flee, but McCall's men, fighting blood up, went right after them. McCall's foreman, Gil Farrow, took a bullet in the chest and toppled sideways, one foot still caught in the stirrup. His horse flung itself around and ran, dragging the dead man with it.

On the edge of the swale, Bateman watched everything unfold before him — unfold and then begin to come apart. They were finished — it didn't take a genius to see that. With a snarl he yanked his reins around and gave the horse his heels.

'Yaaahhhh!'

But even as his horse leapt forward a scared cow lumbered into his path. Horse and cow collided with a solid smack of flesh and Bateman's horse stumbled, reared, unseated him.

Bateman hit the ground awkwardly, dropped his gun, wasted valuable seconds hunting around until he found it again. By then his horse was yards away, spooked by the ongoing crack of

177

gunfire that was following the other rustlers as they too sought to escape in every direction. Bateman ran for the horse, had to stop after a step or two because there were cows everywhere now, lumbering every which-way in their usual ungainly fashion.

Temper slipping, he continued on, more or less shoving cows out of his way. He heard hoofbeats coming closer, turned and threw a shot at the oncoming rider — hatless, he noticed, without really understanding why that should be. A horse went down, its rider spilling to the ground. There was an answering flurry of gunfire. Another cow was hit and dropped with a startled cry.

Bateman made another try for his horse, but now a moving wall of beef separated them, and he knew better than to try and cross it. Instead he changed direction and tried to run for the bushes at the edge of the field.

Riding back straight on his piebald horse, Cyrus McCall spotted him, muttered an oath and went after him at a reckless gallop. As far as he was concerned, no one was going to escape his wrath now, least of all some yellow-livered coward who'd sooner run than fight.

McCall roared, *'Hold it, you varmint!'*

Instead Bateman turned, saw the big rancher bearing down on him, recognized him as much from his bone-white beard as from his husky stature, and quickly fanned his gun. The first shot hit McCall's horse in the chest. It made a high, breathless sound and collapsed, forelegs first. The second shot clipped McCall's right arm, and despite his best efforts he couldn't stop the groan that escaped him.

He went over the horse's head and landed with pain like a lightning-bolt jagging through him. He had no idea how badly he'd been hit. All he knew was that it hurt like a bitch. But that was the thing about McCall; he didn't have any quit in him. He pushed to his feet, right arm hanging loose, unsteady on his feet but now, doggedly, bringing his Colt up, left-handed, to line on Bateman.

Bateman was just about to continue running when he saw McCall climbing back to his feet. He stopped, walked a couple of paces closer to the rancher and snarled, 'Stay down, you old bastard!'

He fired again.

The slug hit McCall in the chest and made him fold and fall again. Nothing existed for him then save a world of hurt, but . . . but . . .

Stubbornly, he turned his head so that he could look up at Bateman.

'Damn you . . .' he managed. 'B . . . best you finish me r . . . right here an' . . . now, mister. 'Cause if you don't — '

Bateman, now standing over him like an angel of death, tightened his lips, thrust the Colt down into McCall's face. 'Consider it done,' he sneered.

A gun-blast ripped through the night and it seemed to McCall that some giant, invisible hand suddenly smacked

Bateman away from him. The rustler landed in a heap six feet away, spurred heels drumming a weird little jig in the earth until he went still with an absolute suddenness that was shocking.

Then someone else was hurrying up from behind McCall, saying, 'Oh my God, Cyrus, what have they done to you — ?'

McCall recognized the voice, looked around and up, saw the shocked, moon-washed face of Simon Doubleday, smelled the powder smoke drifting from the barrel of his borrowed Winchester — the Winchester he'd just used to save McCall's life.

'You!' he rasped. 'Damn it, Doubleday . . . you ain't never gonna let me forget this, are you?'

Then he blacked out.

★　★　★

Shock hung like a pall over Big Sky — over the entire county, if it came to that. After all, this was 1895. Shootouts

181

the like of which happened that night just didn't happen anymore. And yet, as the news spread — thanks in no small part to Simon Doubleday's graphic reportage — the locals had to face the fact that violence could and *did* still happen. Folks might be less than five years away from a new century, but it was obviously taking longer to get the message through to some than it was to others.

Late the following afternoon, in Georgia Lamb's saloon, Val McCall drank his beer without even tasting it. So much had happened in the last sixteen hours that it was hard to take it all in. He'd killed a man. That alone took some getting used to. It didn't matter that he'd done it in defense of his own life; what mattered was that he'd done it, *period*. And then there was his father, looking more like death than death itself, his skin almost as white as his beard, what with all the blood he'd lost.

When the battle was over, the swale

had looked exactly like a battlefield. The bodies of men, cattle and horses lay everywhere. But gradually Val had restored order — with his father gravely wounded and their foreman dead, there'd been nobody else for the job.

The remaining cattle had fled to all points; they'd need rounding up come daylight. In the meantime, there were the rustlers to think about — those few that had survived the fight.

Two of them had tried to argue that they weren't from around those parts and didn't know what they'd been getting themselves into. Predictably, that argument fell on deaf ears. But an older man with gray side-whiskers, who looked like he'd seen it all before, announced that he'd happily spill his guts in return for a little clemency.

Val had been too concerned with his father to pay much attention right then. He'd hated to boost his father up into the saddle of a spare mount like he was a sack of corn, and was afraid that all the bouncing around he was likely to take with every step back to the ranch was more likely to finish him off than the wounds themselves.

But Simon Doubleday, himself somehow numbed by the life he'd taken to save Cyrus McCall from certain death, seemed to welcome the distraction. He'd said, 'What's your name, feller?'

The whiskery man had said, 'Siebert.'

'We can't promise you clemency, Siebert. We're only civilians, we don't have the authority for that. But if I give you my word that I'll stand up for you when it comes to trial — '

'*Don't tell 'em a damn' thing, Will!*' called one of the other prisoners.

But Siebert had other ideas. 'I'd want your word to keep me separate from these here other fellers.'

'*You sonofabitch!*'

'*You're a dead man, Will Siebert!*'

'In the circumstances, I think Sheriff McKenna would agree to that,' Doubleday assured him grimly.

Siebert stared at him in the moonlight. 'Newspaperman, ain't you?' he said. 'Seen you around Singletree before.' His teeth — the few he had left — showed briefly in a cold smile. 'Guess you're hopin' for a story.'

'Much as it pains me to deal with the likes of you,' said Simon, 'I'll do everything I can for you — in return for the truth.'

Siebert spat on his right hand and thrust it out. 'You got a deal, newsman.'

Simon hesitated, then shook with him. 'All right,' he said, 'let's hear it.'

'The man you want,' said Siebert, 'is Fred Lydecker.'

'What? The Sioux Agent up at Green Mountain?'

'Ain't no other,' said Siebert.

'How'd you figure that?'

'I'll tell you.'

So it was that, as soon as Sheriff McKenna heard the news at first light, he paid the Green Mountain Reservation a call and arrested the Indian Agent for his part in the rustling. Lydecker's Sioux wife was inconsolable as McKenna led him back to town in handcuffs.

Meanwhile, Doc Milburn returned from a long and difficult birth down in Avery Crossing only to find himself summoned urgently to Big Sky. Muttering something about there being no rest for the wicked, he arrived at the ranch a little after ten in the morning.

Until he laid eyes on Cyrus McCall, Milburn had convinced himself that nothing could ever kill the rancher. He'd often claimed that McCall was more war-horse than man. But when he entered the rancher's bedroom that morning and saw him laying there, just as pale as chalk, he realized that the unthinkable might just happen after all.

Rachel, Val and one of the longest-serving hands, Amos Lindley, watched as he made a quick preliminary examination of the rancher. McCall lay on his back, eyes closed, brow sweated. Every so often his white beard stirred to the movement of his lips. No one could understand what he was trying to say. He was delirious, so it probably wouldn't have made much sense anyway.

Unable to hold his peace any longer, Val finally stepped forward. 'Is he gonna be all right, Doc?'

He didn't sound like a man right then; he sounded like a scared boy.

Milburn examined the wounds. They had both puffed up around the edges and turned vaguely purple. 'I don't know,' he replied honestly. 'The arm should be easy enough to fix, but . . . well, it all depends on what damage this chest wound has done internally . . . and what damage I'm likely to add when I go in there to get that slug out.' He straightened up, his expression softening when his eyes came to rest on Rachel. 'I'll do what I can for him, you know that. But it's only right you should know the risks, too.'

Rachel accepted that with a single blink, then squared her shoulders. 'He's tough, Ben. Just do what you have to do.'

Beside her, Val swore softly, and this time made no apology for it. 'Damn that Bateman! Simon Doubleday said

187

he was just about to put Pa down like an injured horse!'

'Well, from everything I hear, he got what was coming to him,' said Milburn.

McCall moaned in his restless sleep.

'Amos, give me a hand here. We need to keep him steady. Rachel, I'd appreciate some light over here, while I make a preliminary exploration for the bullet. You got a lamp you can come and hold high?'

'Of course.' She was about to turn away when she caught the way Val was staring down at his father, a look of utter incomprehension on his face. In that moment, everything in her ached for him.

'Val,' she replied, and touched his arm. 'We'll handle things here. You go on into town — '

'I'm not leaving, Ma!'

He wanted to add, *Suppose somethin' goes wrong, and he doesn't make it, and I'm someplace else and don't get the chance to say goodbye?* But he knew that kind of talk wouldn't help anyone, least of all his mother.

'I — '

The look in her eyes silenced further protest. 'The other men've gone into town,' she said. 'After what they went through last night, they're liable to drink too much and cause even more trouble. Best you go in and keep an eye on them.'

He hesitated a moment longer.

'Go on,' she urged. 'Don't worry about your father. He doesn't have the nerve to die on us.'

He looked at her and knew as well as she did that the men would behave themselves in town, but she was trying to give him something to do, other than fret for the life of his father, and for that he appreciated her more than ever.

'All right, Ma. I'll make sure there's no trouble.'

By the time he reached town it was the middle of the afternoon, word — as well as Simon Doubleday's special edition of the *Enterprise* — had already spread far and wide about the shootout, and it was the sole topic of conversation. As Val had entered the saloon, bartender Sam Larch folded his copy of the newspaper, set it aside and wordlessly poured him a beer. Val glanced down at the headline. BIG SKY SETTLES THE SCORE. That much was certainly true. But right then he didn't think they had much to celebrate.

And now here he was, in Georgia Lamb's saloon, drinking beer without tasting it, wondering what was happening back at the ranch, how his father was faring under Doc Milburn's scalpel, whether or not he was still alive —

He hated thinking that way, but couldn't help it. Neither was it doing him any favors sitting here with the rest of the hands who'd taken part in last night's shootout, for the gathering had about it the unmistakable air of a wake.

'Well,' said a wrangler named Jack Elliott, 'his saddle might be empty . . . but not for long.'

'Nothin'll keep that man down,'

agreed Warren Starling. 'Too damn' ornery.'

'He ain't the only one,' said Elliott, trying to lift the mood. 'You got more holes in you than Grandma Small's bloomers, Warren.'

Starling inspected himself briefly. 'That sumbitch with the shotgun all but ruined my wardrobe, that's a fact.'

'Nothin' could ruin *your* wardrobe, pard.'

A half-hearted chuckle went through them, but in truth no one really felt much like laughing just then. As silence settled again over the saloon, the sound of approaching hoofbeats could be heard outside. The animal halted at one of the hitch racks, and a few moments later the batwings pushed open and its rider came inside, his steps unsteady.

The newcomer was Ned Carter.

He stumbled up to the bar and set his elbows on the ringstained wood an instant before his legs could give way beneath him. He'd clearly started drinking early today. If they'd known

191

just how shocked he'd been when he'd learned of Bateman's fate, they'd have understood why. Now he peered down at the newspaper Sam had left on the counter, forcing his bleary eyes to focus.

'Whiskey, Sam,' he slurred.

Sam hesitated. 'Looks like you've already had enough, Ned — '

'*Whiskey*, dammit!'

Sam glanced across at Val and the others, then poured a shot which he slid across to Ned.

Ned slapped coins on the counter, his attention still fixed on the newspaper headline. At last he turned and raised his glass in Val's direction. 'All hail the conquering hero!' he called. ''Big Sky Settles the Score'. And they all return home with nary a scratch . . . well, almost. Five men slung over their saddles, I hear. Five men tied up to boards outside Dellar's funeral parlor for everyone to gawp at! I guess that means they's no need for a judge and jury in Singletree, not when they's a *McCall* around! They settle things their own way — jus' drill 'em and plant 'em.'

Val looked at his one-time friend with a sense of pity he couldn't quite disguise. 'Ned,' he said quietly. 'You're drunk.'

'And you're well on your way,' Ned replied, gesturing to Val's glass. 'I hear one of them bad men darn'-near stopped your pa's clock for him. That's what I hear. The most pow'ful man in Singletree, just this much — ' he held his thumb and forefinger so that they were almost but not quite touching, ' — from meetin' up with Old Nick.'

'*Ned!*'

All eyes turned to Georgia, who had appeared on the gallery above the stage, and was glaring down at him. Her voice was still croaky, and purple bruises where Maggie's fingers had sunk in were still visible at her throat, though she'd tried to hide them with an aptly-named choker.

Ned threw a fuzzy look up at her,

hearing the censure in her tone, instinctively wanting to apologize for his behavior but then thinking, *To hell with it. No one tells me what to do anymore. No one.*

Instead he turned his attention back to Val. 'Why, what will we do if Big Cyrus McCall moves on?' he asked — and giggled.

Sam muttered warningly, 'I think you'd better leave, Ned.' He reached across the counter, intending to shove him toward the exit.

'Don't you touch me!' Ned snarled, and suddenly threw his glass across the room. Val and the others ducked as it flew over their heads and shattered against the wall behind them.

'*Ned!*' Georgia came hurrying down the stairs, the material of her black walking skirt and white Gibson Girl blouse making an angry rustle, her expression tight with fury. 'Get out of here! You can come back when you're sober enough to apologize!'

Ned looked at her, dark eyes bleary

and filled with so much pain that she almost recoiled from it. He looked pale and sweaty, and the upside-down Y-shaped scar sat on his skin like something dark and malignant.

'I'm goin',' Ned replied, and there was a curl to his lip now. 'You won't catch me *dead* in this place again.' He threw another glance at Val. 'See you at your pa's funeral, Val.'

He staggered out, leaving the batwings to flap in his wake.

Temper slipping, Val got to his feet. Jack Elliott immediately reached out and grabbed his wrist. 'Leave it, boy.'

But Val pulled himself free. 'I don't want no trouble,' he replied. 'But I think it's about time Ned and me cleared the air once and for all.'

Georgia took a pace forward. 'Val — '

He ignored her, strode across the room and out onto the boardwalk, where Ned was clumsily trying to step into the stirrup and mount his yellow horse.

'Ned!'

Ned turned, studied him through squinted, bloodshot eyes. 'What the hell do you want? I got nothin' left for you to take. You took it all.'

Pity replaced anger in Val's face, and that, for Ned, was worse.

'We used to be friends, Ned. Could be again. But we need to air this thing between us once and for all.'

'Nothin' to air out,' slurred Ned. 'Big Sky already settled the score.'

'Bateman and his gang got just what they asked for. But that's not what I mean.'

'Then what *do* you mean?'

'Molly Richfield,' said Val. 'Whatever you think me and her got up to behind your back — you're wrong. We didn't get up to nothin'!'

'Is that a fact? Not even — '

'Nothin'!' Val repeated, jaw clenching.

Without warning, Ned turned to face him full on, and his face wrenched out of shape as he yelled, 'You're a *liar*, Val McCall! She played me for a fool, used

196

me to get to *you!* You *both* played me for a fool!'

'That's not right.'

Val heard Georgia push through the Bar D hands clustered in the saloon doorway behind him, heard her high heels on the boardwalk. 'Ned . . . ' she began, her voice low, scared.

Ned ignored her, kept his bleary eyes fixed on Val. 'You didn't even *want* her, did you?' he accused. 'But you didn't want me to have her, either!' He stabbed a finger at his scarred face. 'So you both left me marked for the rest of my life!'

He drew his Colt.

It was the fastest thing Val had ever seen. Immediately he raised his hands. '*Hey, now!* Put that damn' smoke wheel away, Ned!'

But the curl to Ned's lip grew more pronounced, and did ugly things to his scar. He thumbed back the hammer and squeezed the trigger. The boom of the sound echoed from one end of town to the other, and instinctively Val flinched, but the shot went wide; Ned was so drunk and so distraught that he hadn't even bothered to take aim.

'Ned!' It was Georgia. And then, 'Val . . . Val, don't crowd him . . . come back here.'

Nothing would have suited Val better than to take Georgia's advice, but the mood Ned was in right then, he was as much a danger to himself as anyone else, and that meant that Val had no choice; if he wanted to calm his one-time friend down, he had to put himself in the line of fire.

'Ned . . . listen, now . . . it doesn't — '

'I've always been your fool!' Ned sobbed.

And fired again.

Georgia screamed as the bullet tore a crease through Val's shoulder. Val staggered a little, felt something warm spilling down the inside of his shirtsleeve, and was too shocked in that moment to wonder just how badly he'd been hurt.

'Well,' said Ned, and he was crying now, big, silver tears rolling down his cheeks, 'it's time this fool burnt his prince down!'

As he stabbed the Colt at Val, Val's thoughts started tumbling over each other. *No . . . no . . . he means it . . . he's going to kill you unless . . . no . . . no . . .*

But he was already acting. He dropped to one knee, hooked his Colt from leather, brought it up, his mind still whirling —

Georgia screamed, 'No! Val — no!'

. . . wound him if you can . . . don't kill him . . .

— the gun bucked against his fist like a living thing, jerked a little to the left, and beyond the sudden pall of gun smoke he saw Ned lurch, thought, *I got him*, and then, *but how bad?*

Ned came up against his palomino. The horse sidestepped and then Ned fell forward, hunched up, seeming almost to hug himself. Even as Val shoved his gun away, Georgia ran past him, was there as Ned fell loosely at her feet. She dropped down beside him, slid a trembling arm under Ned's now hatless head for support.

Ned, hardly seeming to know he was there, gave a sudden, bubbly cough. Blood erupted from his mouth, hit her white blouse, spilled down his chin in a thick red wash. A sob tugged at Georgia.

Val sank to one knee beside her, numb, helpless and baffled by what had just happened. The wound, he saw, was bad, real bad; and knowing that, knowing that everything had just gotten even worse than it already was, Val felt hopelessly out of his depth.

'Ned . . . oh God, man . . . I didn't want for this to h-happen . . . '

As he tore off his bandanna and tried to staunch the blood, he heard Georgia praying in an undertone. Ned, staring up at the sky, eyes seeming to glaze even as Val stared into them, murmured, 'Still your . . . '

'Just set still till help gets here.'

But Val knew help was not going to get there. Doc Milburn was tending his pa right now — assuming his pa was still alive for the tending.

Ned coughed blood again. It might have been a trick of the light, but already the color had leeched from his face. He looked gray now, an impossible color for human skin. The blood, bright red in contrast, glistened in the late afternoon sunlight. And Ned's scar, too, seemed to stand out, like something charred and rotten.

Val realized then that Ned had come back from wherever he'd gone. He looked into Ned's eyes, saw pain there, and sorrow, and hatred.

'Still your fool . . . ' Ned managed.

Then he went still.

He was dead.

And though he hadn't meant to, though it was the last thing he had wanted to do or thought he would *ever* do, Val McCall had killed him.

11

'Man *that is born of woman hath but
a short time to live, and is full of
misery . . . '*

Maggie Carter barely heard the
words. She'd been in a state of shock
ever since Val McCall had brought Ned
home three days earlier; Ned, wrapped
in a coarse woolen blanket, thrown
across the saddle of his beloved yellow
horse, stained with blood, stinking of it.

' *. . . he cometh up and is cut down
like a flower . . . '*

Try as she might, she simply could
not allow herself to believe that this was
anything more than a particularly vivid
nightmare. And yet no nightmare had
ever been filled with such detail: the
sight of Val McCall leading the horse up
to the rack in front of the house; dread
settling like lead shot in her stomach;
the silence that suddenly descended

over the ranch, when not even the dogs barked. She remembered being called by Hester, coming out into the sunshine and knowing, just knowing, that something was wrong, because what with one thing and another there always seemed to be something wrong these days . . . but never had she expected . . . this.

Kate had come out to join her. The girl had been quiet and withdrawn following Nubbs's sudden departure. Maggie had no idea whether or not her daughter had believed her when she'd said that for some time now Nubbs had been hinting that he'd been getting fiddle-footed and wanted to move on. It was the best she could come up with at the time.

First Nubbs. Now Ned.

Kate's fist rose to her mouth as Val McCall stepped lifelessly from his saddle and handed the reins to Ned's horse across to Wade Palmer. He looked at them then; Maggie saw that his eyes were red from shed tears, but that cut no ice with her. He hadn't wept for what he'd done — he wept for what he feared the consequences might be.

'In the midst of life we be in death: of whom may we seek for succor but of thee, O Lord, which for our sins justly art displeased . . . '

Maggie had come down off the porch, approached the blanket-wrapped body almost reluctantly. Ned's gun belt — black leather, with a silver star attached to the holster, had been buckled and hung over his pommel. Hardly seeing that, other than to acknowledge that it was the gun that had brought him to grief, she'd reached out, closed her fingers on the edge of the blanket —

'I wouldn't, Mrs. Carter.'

That had been Val. Ignoring him, she'd pulled back the blanket and —

She had known then that it wasn't a dream.

Had it not been for the blood at his mouth, not quite cleaned away before they'd wrapped him and brought him home, he might have been a little boy again, sleeping.

Instead he was cold, pale, still. Dead.

There'd been a half-hearted attempt to explain what had happened. Val claimed he had a whole townful of witnesses to say that he'd acted in self-defense. Maggie didn't believe a word of it. Singletree was a town ruled by the McCalls. They'd say whatever the McCalls wanted them to say.

' . . . *but spare us Lord most holy, O God most mighty, O holy and merciful savior, thou most worthy judge eternal, suffer us not at our last hour for any pains of death to fall from thee.*'

It didn't seem right. Here they were, burying her boy — her *boy!* — while Cyrus McCall, who'd taken two bullets that night he and his men had braced the rustlers, was said to be making a slow but steady recovery.

She drew herself up. She hadn't cried when Val brought Ned home, and she didn't intend to cry now, as they buried him. She was not one for that. She simply wouldn't allow it. But beside her, Kate cried softly, stopping only once, to look behind her as if she felt she were being watched.

Maybe they were, though she couldn't think by whom. The funeral was strictly a ranch affair. No one else had been invited. Even Georgia Lamb had known better that to show her face.

'Forasmuch as it hath pleased Almighty God of his great mercy to take until himself the soul of our dear brother here departed . . . '

Maggie allowed herself the softest sigh as Wade Palmer and the ranch hands who had been closest to Ned lowered his coffin into the ground, no more than six feet from where her husband had lain these past two years. Kate's shoulders hitched, and Maggie knew she should comfort her, but somehow couldn't bring herself to move.

' . . . we therefore commit his body to the ground, earth to earth, ashes to ashes, dust to dust, in sure and certain hope of the resurrection to eternal life,

through our Lord Jesus Christ . . . '

And then, at last, it was over. The men clapped their hats back on, Reverend Braxton came over to offer his condolences and then shuffled off in the direction of his buggy. Singly and in groups, the mourners left the picket-fenced cemetery. Silence not even broken by birdsong descended. And then, a figure finally broke cover from the stand of trees in which he had watched the entire service.

Val McCall let himself through the low gate, stood at the head of the new grave and looked at the marker for a long time. He felt as if he should say something, but right then he didn't have any words to express how he really felt. All he could do was stand there, and look down at the grave, and remember the friendship he and Ned had enjoyed, and feel sick that it should have ended the way it did.

'You shouldn't have come here, Val.'

He heeled around fast; quickly, guiltily, dashed the tears from eyes that were underslung with dark, haunted circles. Kate was standing just the other side of the fence, her face a ghostly contrast to her all-black outfit.

'I . . . I had to,' he managed at last.

'Conscience?' she asked, but almost immediately regretted it. 'I'm sorry. After the inquest I guess we all know how it was.'

'I went after Ned to clear the air,' Val replied. 'Please believe that, Kate. He was drunk, he was hurting. But . . . '

'What?'

He gestured irritably. 'It don't make sense.'

'What doesn't?'

'I don't know . . . there was something else eating at Ned that day; more than just Molly Richfield. Something deep. I just don't know what.'

'Well, you'd best know this,' said Kate. 'There are some wounds that time simply cannot heal, and my mother has yet to shed a tear. So you'd best be gone, Val. And . . . ' She looked at him with a sadness he could hardly bear to acknowledge. 'And if you know what's good for you,' she finished, 'don't ever set foot on Carter land again.'

★   ★   ★

In the weeks following Ned's funeral, something in Maggie died. She'd come from great hardship to marry the man of her dreams. Together they'd built something for their future. But Charlie Carter hadn't had a future.

Nubbs had been the next one to go, though no one save Maggie knew or even suspected why. Of all the people around her, Nubbs had been the one she had felt completely able to trust.

Now Nubbs was gone . . . and so was Ned.

Guilt also played its part in her slow but steady deterioration, though even in her darkest moments she refused to believe that she had tried to shape Ned into something he could never hope to be. No: there was another reason for the way Ned had ended up, and someone else to blame. Someone whom she finally decided she should use to restore some . . . balance . . . to her world.

In the days following Ned's funeral, Maggie kept mostly to herself. She took her meals in her room, though she ate little. She spoke rarely, content, it seemed, to let Wade Palmer run the ranch on her behalf. Word eventually reached her that Cyrus McCall had ordered his fences to be taken down immediately now that the rustlers had been dealt with. The news should have pleased her. Instead it meant nothing. As far as she was concerned, the damage had already been done.

At last she left her room to ride into Singletree, right past the very spot just outside Georgia Lamb's saloon where Ned had bled out his life, and on to the U.S. Post Office. Here she mailed the letter she had thought long and hard about writing, which carried an address in South Dakota.

After that she returned to the ranch to sit . . . and await a response.

One early evening about two weeks later, she was running numbers at her desk, allowing instinct to dictate her actions because concentration had become too difficult of late. Her door was ajar and Kate, in the hallway outside, stood for a time, watching her mother with clear concern. Maggie seemed entirely unaware of her presence.

For a moment Kate wondered if she should say something, to try and get her mother to open up to her much as she had once hoped to get Ned to confide in her, too. It had now been a month since Ned's death, and as far as she knew Maggie had yet to shed a tear. To keep so much hurt bottled up inside her was wrong.

But even as she considered it, she knew how Maggie would react. *Thank you for your concern, Kathryn, but there's no need to worry about me, I'm fine.*

In other words, *Mind your own beeswax.*

Even so, she went closer, knocked softly at the door and then went in without waiting to be invited. 'Busy, Mother?' She knew it was a ridiculous thing to say, but she had to say *something* to open a conversation.

'I'm always busy,' Maggie replied without looking up.

'I'd be happy to stay and help, if you like.'

'No,' Maggie said shortly. 'It will take longer to show you what needs doing than to sit here and do it all myself.'

'Nevertheless,' persisted Kate, 'I've got to learn. One day all this will be my responsibility, remember.'

Finally Maggie looked up at her, her face as unreadable as ever. 'You've made up your mind, then? To continuing building what your father and I started?'

'I believe I have, yes.'

'Very well,' said Maggie, and bent her head to her figures again.

'I thought you'd be pleased,' said Kate.

'So did I,' Maggie replied. 'But now . . . ' She made a vague motion with the hand holding the pen. 'Now I wonder if the price we paid for building this place came too high.'

'I never thought I'd hear you say that about the C.A. Carter.'

'Nevertheless, you have. Was it worth all the loss, the pain, to build something that now seems so . . . worthless?'

'You're tired, Mother. Worse, you're overtired, and not thinking clearly. We should go to St. Louis together. I'll show you all the sights — but I guarantee you'll be chafing at the bit to get back to the — '

She stopped as something caught her eye through the window behind Maggie — someone riding slump-shouldered into the darkening yard.

'There's a man riding in,' she said, and Maggie's head suddenly snapped up from the ledger, her face showing true animation for the first time in weeks. 'I don't know him . . . '

'I do,' said Maggie, rising now. 'Go to your room, Kathryn.'

'What?'

'I would as soon see this man alone,' Maggie explained.

'But — '

'He is a cattle buyer with a reputation for hard bargaining,' Maggie cut in tersely. 'I want neither interruption nor distraction while I deal with him.'

Kate held her stare for a long beat, not knowing why the statement should make her feel so uneasy.

'Go,' said Maggie.

Much as she didn't want to leave right then, Kate knew better than to argue. With a nod, she went to her room and left Maggie alone.

Maggie stood listening. At the front of the house she heard the newcomer draw rein, dismount. It was only when she heard Kate close her bedroom door behind her that Maggie finally hurried downstairs, a curious mixture of feelings warring within her.

She stopped at the front door, hesitated. It would be so easy to leave it shut, to call through to the man on the other side that she'd changed her mind and that he wasn't welcome here after all and never would be.

Instead, she opened the door and looked up into the battered face of Abraham Tanner.

'You'd better come inside,' she said.

With a brusque nod, her stepfather — the same stepfather she'd once shot — brushed past her, into the house.

★   ★   ★

In the parlor, as he studied Charles's collection of long guns in the rack behind the door, she in turn studied him.

Time had not treated Abraham Tanner kindly. He was whiskery, and his intemperate ways had left him ravaged. His eyes were a dark hazel, their whites shot through with blood.

His nose, once broken, had never been reset. It was flanked by pronounced ridges of cheekbone, beneath which the cheeks themselves were hollow, scored with the deep-etched lines of a life lived hard. His mouth was wide, the lips thin, twisted into a constant, cruel sneer. He was, she supposed, about sixty now, and at first glance he appeared to be a wreck. And yet, when she looked closer, she saw that he still stood tall, an inch, maybe two, above six feet. And beneath his well-worn clothes — a black frock coat that hung to the ankles of his knee-high preacher boots, a green Flanagan shirt with a greasy tab collar tucked into walnut-brown field trousers held up by black suspenders — he had retained his powerful build.

He took off his black hat. Beneath it, he wore his iron-gray hair long and unkempt, finger-brushed carelessly back off a high, lined forehead. And around his hips was buckled a plain leather gun belt, in the pocket of which sat a Smith & Wesson Schofield .44.

At last she said, 'I almost thought you wouldn't come.'

He looked back at her with contempt in his eyes. 'I was hardly likely to refuse,' he finally rasped. 'You made it pretty clear what you'd do if I *didn't* come.'

'The law?'

'The law,' he said. 'Anyway — I'm here. What I want to know now is why? Comes to that, how did you even manage to *find* me?'

She couldn't deny it; she was as scared of him now as she had ever been, because she sensed that age had done nothing to soften him, to invest within him any semblance of compassion. He was the same hard, unyielding, violent man he'd always been, the same man who had raped her once and then taken a bullet when he'd tried it again.

Nevertheless, she masked her fear as best she could. 'I've made it my business to know where you were every day for the last twenty-five years,' she said.

'Why?'

She hesitated a moment. Then: 'You owe me, Abraham Tanner.'

'The hell I do.'

'You *owe* me,' she repeated. 'You made life hell for my mother and I, with your wicked ways. And I knew that one day you'd pay for it.'

He rubbed at his left arm. 'I've *already* paid for it. This damn' arm's never been the same since you put a ball in it.'

'Nevertheless, a debt is a debt.'

'Well, I'm right sorry to disappoint you, Margaret, but I don't have anythin',' he replied. 'Any case, you seem to be doin' just fine without *my* money.'

'It's not money I'm interested in.'

'Then what is it?'

'I know every jail and cesspool town you've lived in since Tennessee,' she said. 'And I know you're not afraid to use that gun you still wear.'

He frowned down at her, suddenly curious. 'What is it you *want*, girl?'

She didn't answer immediately. It still wasn't too late. She could still back out.

But she said it anyway.

'I want a man to die.'

For a few seconds he just stared at her. Then, to her annoyance, he laughed coolly. 'I'm not a killer for hire — '

'No? What about Morgan Fitzhugh? Sam Flowers? John Westcott?'

'They never gave me any option.'

'Are you going to tell me they all drew on you first?'

There was no point in denying it. He could see that she'd done her research.

'Listen, Margaret . . . whatever it is you got in mind . . . I don't do things like that anymore.'

'You'd shoot a man for the pleasure of seeing him fall,' she said with disdain. 'Don't deny it.'

'Well, there's one thing you can take to the bank. I sure don't kill without *reason.*'

'You want a reason?' she countered. 'I'll give you one. The man I want you to kill shot and killed my son in cold blood, and brought him back here slung over his saddle.'

'That's no reason. Your son's nothin' to me.'

'That,' she replied, and there was a curious satisfaction in her as she said it, 'is where you're wrong. Ned was raised a Carter — I made sure of that. But as much as it sickens me to say it . . . he was born a Tanner.'

He stared down at her, as if having trouble understanding exactly what she was saying.

'When I fled your house that night,' Maggie continued venomously, 'I was carrying your child. Oh, no one knew the truth but me. But now you have reason enough, I think.'

He shook his head. 'You're lyin'. It can't be. I . . . I — '

She turned, snatched up a framed daguerreotype of Ned that usually sat on the small table between the two windows and handed it to him. He took it almost against his will. The picture showed Ned before the accident, a nice, upstanding young man who . . . who . . .

Who looked the spitting image of Abraham Tanner when he was that age.

Tanner swallowed softly, unsure just how he should feel. A son? A *son?* And all these years, he'd never even known he had the one thing every man hopes for? It didn't seem fair. Still, little in his life had *ever* been fair. But if he'd known he had a son, if he'd had a son to look up to him, then things might have been a whole lot different. *He'd* have been a whole lot different.

He thought of all the years he'd squandered, all the years he'd lost because of the bottle. He looked again at the daguerreotype and something in him ached because he wanted to know the boy who looked back at him, he wanted to set him on a better path than the one he'd taken, and now he knew that was never going to happen.

'How . . . ' He licked his lips, started again. 'Who killed him, an' why?'

Maggie told him. Leastways, she told

him how it was as *she* saw it. Neither did she neglect to mention just how rich and powerful the McCalls were, for she knew he had always hated what he saw as the arrogance of the wealthy. He'd often ranted about how they'd put him down his whole life, had blamed them for his drinking, claiming that it blotted out the humiliation he'd suffered at their hands.

Now she opened a drawer, took from it an envelope that she thrust at him. 'Everything you need to know is in here,' she said, low-voiced. 'His name, where to find him, the kind of schedule he runs to. Learn it, destroy it, and then put the knowledge I have given you to the right use.'

Tanner weighed the envelope thoughtfully.

'I want this to square us,' he said after a long pause.

'It will square things with your *son*,' she said.

'But not with you?'

'You will never square things with

222

me, Abraham Tanner,' she replied. Then: 'When it's done, leave. And if I ever lay eyes on you again, I'll kill you.'

His eyes leapt from the envelope to her face, and the evil she saw in them almost made her take a step away from him. His mouth stirred, his teeth showed fleetingly, and then, rattler-swift, his right hand shot out and his fingers clamped around her throat.

'Don't threaten me, Margaret,' he said. 'We both know you don't have the guts to follow it through.'

He kept his hand around her throat for a moment longer, then released her. Fear warred with anger inside her, and fear won — the same fear she'd known all those years ago, and which she had felt sure she would never experience again.

'Can I keep the picture?' he asked.

She inclined her head. 'I . . . I have another.'

He nodded, took it. 'All right, Margaret. I'll handle it. But it won't be pretty.'

'I don't expect it to be.'

'I mean . . . I'm older now, slower . . . I brace this feller in a stand-up fight, he's as likely to kill me as I am to kill him.'

'Then don't give him that chance.'

'You mean, back-shoot him?'

'No.' She was definite on this point. 'I don't care how you do it, but he has to know *why* he's to die.'

He looked down at her, appearing suddenly, genuinely puzzled. 'What happened to you?' he asked. 'There was a time when you was so soft and sweet.'

'You want to know what happened to me?' she countered. And then she hissed: '*You.*'

12

That night Tanner sat beside a small, wind-whipped fire in the shadow of Eagle's Nest and tilted the picture of Ned toward the flames. He still couldn't believe the likeness. It was like looking in the mirror. Except that this younger, innocent version of Abraham Tanner could possibly have gone in a different, better direction and made himself a different and better kind of life, if only he'd known his real father . . . and if only he'd lived.

If only he'd lived.

Tanner couldn't believe how angry Ned's death made him feel. He'd never been a sentimental man. There'd never been any room in his life for that. It had been a hard life, and he'd grown bark on him in order to survive it. But he was an older man now, and the idea that he'd had a son he'd never known and now never *would* know . . . it seemed so . . . unjust . . . and it brought back memories of all the other unjust things that had shaped him over the years.

At first he'd tried to tell himself that the boy was nothing to him. How could he be? He'd never known him, never spoken to him. He was a stranger. But that wasn't the point. He was *kin*. And the way Margaret told it, he'd been shot down in cold blood by a boy who'd claimed to be his friend. No one, *no one*, did that to a Tanner without paying the price.

He felt a restlessness in him then that he hadn't felt in years, and knew he wouldn't get any peace until he did as Margaret had said, and settled the score. So, as the night grew older, he slowly, painstakingly studied the map she'd drawn for him that showed the Big Sky ranch and its surroundings, and the rough timetable she'd sketched out — presumably based upon her own observations — that told him all he needed to know about the McCalls and their movements.

It seemed that Val's father was still recovering from gunshot wounds he'd sustained in a fight with rustlers. The McCalls were tough, then, and they dispensed their own brand of justice. He'd remember that.

After a time his eyes began to ache and he methodically fed all the information into the fire and watched it crisp and burn. He was still numb with the idea that he'd had a son. As far as he was concerned, it was one more lost opportunity in a lifetime that had been filled with them. And the more he thought about that, the more he began to long for a bottle, and in the end the craving he'd believed he'd put behind him years ago grew so strong again that he saddled up and headed for Singletree, there to buy one.

★ ★ ★

For the next several days Tanner alternately drank and haunted the timbered hills around Big Sky, watching the place through an old brass telescope he'd always carried with him. The ranch was orderly and functional, the big house, bunkhouse, corrals and out-buildings just as spruce as could be. He looked at the stock — crossbred Braham shorthorns, good, hardy stock. Eventually he identified Val McCall from the description Maggie had given him. He was of an age with Ned, he saw. Trouble was, he was nearly always surrounded by hired hands, among whom he seemed to be mighty popular. There was never any chance to get him alone.

Winter was coming and the days were growing short and cold. Tanner froze and his ageing bones hated it. The evenings were even worse. He figured he must be getting soft. But one thing helped to keep out the chill, and that was whiskey. Somewhere along the line he'd tried to give it up, and he'd made a pretty good fist of it. Now, though . . . He'd forgotten how good it could taste, how well it could slake a man's thirst and help him blot out all the things he'd sooner forget.

But time was wasting. And though he'd kidded himself that he could handle the whiskey, that it was just for medicinal purposes, he feared what might happen if he stayed out here much longer, and got to rely on it all over again.

He had to act, then — and fast. Get the job done and clear the territory, go back up to Dakota and pick up his life as if nothing had happened. But first, he needed to get Val McCall alone, on ground of his own choosing.

The opportunity came two mornings later. While Tanner was watching the house through an old brass telescope he'd taken off a dead Indian years before, a buckboard was prepared for travel and brought around to the front of the big house by a hired man. A short time later an attractive, raven-haired woman Tanner had already identified as Val's mother, Rachel

McCall, came out onto the porch, resplendent in a brown tapestry coat, at the hem of which could be seen a full navy wool skirt. A big, heavyset man with a white beard followed her out, moving awkwardly and leaning on a cane. There couldn't be too many bulls like that in these parts — he had to be Val's father, Cyrus, still recovering from his wounds.

Tanner studied them intently through the old telescope.

Husband and wife spoke briefly. Tanner's mouth twisted into a sour grin as he imagined what they were saying. The wife would be nagging her man, as wives did: *Now remember what I said. You just rest up. Go anywhere near a horse and you'll have me to answer to.*

Sure enough, Cyrus McCall made an irritable gesture with his free hand, then turned and hobbled back inside.

Rachel climbed up onto the seat beside the hired man. He looked old, stooped, with a walrus moustache and no fight in him worth a damn.

Tanner saw it all in his mind, then — how he could achieve what needed to be done.

He backed out of the brush, scurried down-slope to his waiting liver chestnut horse, shoved the telescope into a scuffed saddlebag and then mounted up.

By the time he reached his destination — a well-timbered slope overlooking the trail about halfway to Singletree — the buckboard was just coming around a distant bend. Tanner sat his horse in tree-shadow for a while, watching it come closer, then set heels to his horse and went down the slope to meet it.

As he closed on the wagon, he raised one hand to flag it down. Seeing no reason for suspicion, the hired man — his name was Lyle Eggers — hauled on the reins and slowed the vehicle as Tanner brought his horse to a halt beside him.

'Help you, mister?'

Tanner nodded. 'Sure can,' he said.

Then he leaned sideways out of the

saddle and punched Eggers straight in the face.

As the elderly ranch-hand slumped back against Rachel, she cried out in surprise and instinctively reached for the injured man. The blow had knocked him silly, and broken his nose. Now the entire lower half of his face was awash with blood.

Rachel's head snapped toward him, and there was fury in her but not much in the way of fear. Tanner liked that, liked knowing he would teach her the meaning of fear before this was over.

'What — ?'

As she struggled to sit forward, he slid his Colt from leather. Guessing he was after robbing them, Eggers husked, 'You sonofabitch!' And Rachel herself quickly untangled the tapestry bag from her wrist and threw it to the ground beside the wagon.

'Here,' she said. 'It's all I've got.'

Tanner looked at her and chuckled. He'd forgotten just how alive a man could feel when he held the upper hand, the power. 'I don't want that,' he replied. Then: 'Get down, lady.'

'What?'

'*Get down off that damn wagon!* And *you* — ' addressing Eggers, 'Soon as your head clears, you get on back to the ranch, and deliver this message to Val McCall.'

What he said next made Rachel's blood run cold.

★ ★ ★

Cyrus McCall was dozing in a chair by the window when he heard voices as if from a long ways off. He stirred with a half-snore and opened his eyes. He was the parlor's sole occupant, so he guessed he must have been dreaming.

For a moment he forgot himself and stretched farther than his healing wounds would allow. He winced and swore. Lord, he hated being an invalid. All he'd ever known was the hard, physical life of a rancher. Even when he'd started making real money, enough to pay other men to do all the work for him, he'd still labored from dawn till dusk, because he wanted to. Ever since he'd been shot, though, he'd been forced to take it easy, and he detested it.

He heard voices again, drifting in from the yard. He still couldn't make out what was being said, but there was something vaguely urgent about the tone. Carefully he edged forward in his chair, peered through the window.

Val was out there, holding his horse by its cheek strap, talking animatedly with Lyle Eggers. A handful of hired men had also gathered around the buckboard Eggers had just tooled into the yard.

That's when he knew something was wrong.

Eggers was supposed to be taking Rachel into Singletree today. They'd only left thirty minutes earlier, and weren't expected back until late this afternoon. Aside from that, Eggers was holding his face, and now that McCall looked a little closer, he could see that the man was bleeding from the nose.

Panic gripped him immediately. There'd been an accident! And Rachel . . . ?

He snatched up his cane and lumbered out onto the porch. 'What is it?' he called gruffly. 'What's happened, Lyle?'

As all eyes turned toward him, Val broke away from the group, leaving his mount ground-hitched. He said, 'It's all right, Pa, just — '

'What's happened, dammit?'

Val let air go through his nose. 'Someone's took Ma,' he said at last.

McCall swayed a little. '*What?* What do you mean, *taken* her?'

'Man came out of nowhere, broke Lyle's nose, took Ma and said if we want her back, I'm to go up to Eagle's Nest.'

Cyrus pushed past him, mind whirling. 'She's been kidnapped?' he asked Eggers.

'Yessir. There was nothin' I could — '

'And they want me to pay to get her back?'

'No, Pa,' said Val, catching up with him as he closed on the group around the buckboard. 'You're not listenin'. This man, whoever he is, he wants *me*. Alone — and he's usin' Ma to get me!'

For a moment the older man's face was blank as he struggled to understand this sudden turn of events. Then something in his expression hardened.

'Maggie Carter,' he said in a near whisper.

Val scowled. 'Maggie? You mean because of . . . '

He still couldn't bring himself to say *Ned*.

McCall snarled simply, 'Eye for an eye.'

An angry buzz went through the assembled hands.

'No, Pa. You got to be wrong.'

'I doubt it. Why else do you suppose she didn't press charges at the time? 'Cause she figured to settle things her own way, that's why! And where better to do it? Eagle's Nest overlooks the Carter place.' Then: 'Slim — you tend

236

to Lyle, here. Fletch — saddle me a horse.'

'No, Pa! He wants me, alone. We don't do what he says, he'll kill Ma for sure.'

'He'd better damn' well not.'

'Well, that's a chance I'm not prepared to take! 'Sides, you ain't sat a saddle in weeks.'

'I'll slow you down, is that it?'

'Pa, I ain't got the time to argue about it.'

McCall reached for him, tightened fingers around his arm. 'You go in there alone, you're a sitting duck! Only one way in or out.'

'We'll see about that,' said Val, and pulling away, he stepped up to the saddle and gathered his reins.

'What does that mean?'

'He wants me, he can have me,' Val replied. 'But first, I got to know somethin'.'

He gave the horse his spurs and the animal shot out of the yard as if scalded.

McCall watched him go, maybe watched him go for the very last time. Temper flaring, he wheeled on the men, who all but recoiled from him. 'Are you still here?' he barked. 'Fletch — get me that damn' horse!'

Fletch hesitated.

'I said get me that damn' horse!' McCall repeated. And then, before the waddy could do anything about it, McCall wrenched the man's Colt from its high holster and stuffed it into his waistband. 'Do it, damn you — *now!*'

13

His mind in turmoil, Val did the only thing he could right then — he tried to make sense of what had happened. And the only way he could do that was to confront Maggie Carter. If his pa was right, and Maggie *had* hired this killer, maybe he could appeal to her to call him off.

He held his horse to a speed that was little short of reckless, knowing he should show more caution but unable to right then. At length he came through a trail between two steep hills and spotted a rider in the distance, recognizing Kate and Whiskey immediately.

He turned his mount toward them, yelled Kate's name. She heard him, caught the urgency in his tone, turned in her saddle and came to meet him.

When he was close enough he drew

to a halt and gasped, 'Is your mother up at the ranch?'

He looked terrible. 'Yes,' she said, frowning. 'But like I told you before, Val, you're not welcome here.'

'Hell with that!' he said. 'You know what she's done? Leastways, what I *think* she's done? She's hired some damn' gunman to kidnap my mother so's he can get me up to Eagle's Nest and kill me!'

The color leached from her face. 'What makes you think . . . ?'

'Oh, come off it, Kate!' he snapped. 'You said it yourself — 'Some wounds simply won't heal.''

'Don't be ridiculous,' she said, but there was no conviction in the denial, and even in his present state he was quick to spot it.

'You know something, don't you?' he said.

'No . . . '

'What is it?'

She shook her head. 'There was a man here . . . a few days ago. He

240

showed up after dark — '

'What did he look like?'

'I didn't see him clearly. She wouldn't let me. She said he was a cattle buyer and I wasn't to interrupt her — '

As far as Val was concerned, that clinched it. 'Dammit, Kate — she was hiring this gunman or whatever the heck he is!'

She wanted to deny the charge, but couldn't. Why else had her mother been so secretive? And yet she could hardly believe that Maggie would really go to such desperate lengths to —

'Go find her, Kate,' Val said, and it was more beg than request. 'Make her turn this thing around before it's too late.'

She looked into his face, his eyes, and she felt everything that he was feeling in that moment — hurt, confusion, dread.

'I'll do it,' she said. 'What about you?'

'I ain't got much choice. I got to give myself up so he'll release my ma.'

'But if you're right, he'll *kill* you.'

'He'll try. What I got to do when I get up there is make sure he don't succeed.'

* * *

In her little office-cum-bedroom, Maggie knew that something was wrong the minute she saw Kate gallop into the yard. It must be wrong, for she would never push Whiskey that way if everything was all right.

She thought about Abraham Tanner — she'd thought about little else over the past few days — and told herself, *He's done it. He's killed Val McCall and Kate just got the news.*

Her eyelids fluttered briefly. It was done, then. Ned could rest easy at last. And yet the knowledge gave her no satisfaction, and even less peace of mind.

She heard the front door open, heard footsteps climbing the stairs in a hurry and composed herself as best she could. A few seconds later the door opened — no knock this time, she noted — and

Kate came in and glared down at her.

For a moment there was only silence. She tried to read Kate's expression but it was impossible. Then Kate said, 'That man who showed up here a few nights ago . . . who was he?'

It wasn't a question she'd been expecting. 'I told you. He was a cattle buyer from — '

'He was a hired killer, wasn't he?'

Maggie began to feel growing unease. She wondered if Tanner's mission had gone wrong, and that he had died instead of Val McCall. Strangely, that thought *did* bring a sense of satisfaction.

'I hope you're not calling me a liar,' she bluffed.

'I'm sorry, Mother, but I am,' Kate replied. 'Rachel McCall's been abducted, and if Val doesn't go to Eagle's Nest this man, whoever he is, will kill her.'

Maggie didn't want to react, but it was there on her face before she could disguise it. '*What?*'

'This man . . . you hired him for this, didn't you?'

'Of course not!'

'Then who was that man the other night? Why so much secrecy over a 'cattle buyer'?'

Maggie turned away from her, put her eyes back on the ranch beyond the window. 'I'm sorry for Rachel McCall, of course I am,' she said, and she was. 'But whatever happens to that family, you can be sure they've brought it on themselves.'

She felt Kate's eyes burning into her. 'Mother, you can't take the law into your own hands! Val killed Ned in self-defense — everyone said so. He did what anyone else would have done in the same situation. Why can't you accept that? Because he's a *McCall?*'

'Stay out of this, Kathryn! It's none of our business!'

'Mother . . . please . . . it's not too late. It's not too late to stop it! And if you won't, *I* will!'

Maggie turned on her. 'What do you mean by that?'

'I'm a Carter, Mother,' Kate replied,

almost grinding out the words. 'A Carter hired this . . . this killer. Now we'll see if a Carter can call him off!'

'You can't go up there!' Maggie said, rising, green eyes wide now. 'You can't risk your life for the McCalls!'

'Someone's got to. Someone's got to bring this madness to an end once and for all!'

She stormed out of the room. A moment later she reappeared in the yard, and Maggie heard her call: 'Wade! I need a fast horse — *now!* Go saddle Sundown for me!'

★　★　★

The minute Val rode into the shadow of the mountain, the temperature dropped like a stone. Then again, maybe it was the sense of dread that had continued building in him after he'd left Kate Carter that made him shiver; the knowledge that he was playing for a stake higher even than his own life — the life of his mother. If anything went wrong, if he misjudged one step of his hastily-constructed plan . . .

But he couldn't afford to think that way. Instead he drew rein and studied the mountain before him. It was a sprawling, chaotic jumble of limestone rock scored through with canyons and caves and sharp, killer drop-offs. It shelved progressively higher from both east and west until it formed the towering central peak known as Eagle's Nest. Behind that, gray clouds scudded north on a biting wind.

He scoured the ranks of low-hanging pine and aspen that covered its elevations, the bare mountain passes in between, which led nowhere. And again he thought about what his father had said.

You go in there alone, you're a sitting duck. Only one way in or out.

It was common knowledge that, while a number of trails led toward that rocky summit, only one would take him right to the peak itself.

But Val knew different.

There was another way to approach the peak, this one from the north. Billy Broken Hand had shown it to him years ago — to him, Ned and Kate, now that he thought on it. If he could just remember the way, it was possible that he could come out above and behind the man who'd kidnapped his mother. And if he could do that, then just maybe he could get the drop on the sonofabitch before —

But there was nothing to be gained by sitting here thinking about it. His mother was up there right now, and it tore at him to think what she must be going through, what she'd already endured . . . and what still might come.

He put heels to the horse and started up into the high country.

⋆ ⋆ ⋆

'What do you want?' asked Rachel McCall.

She didn't really expect an answer, but she had to do something to break the absolute isolation of the mountain peak — and relieve the tension that had been building in her ever since this nameless man had come into her life and kidnapped her.

Black frock coat flapping around him like the restless wings of some monstrous bat, Abraham Tanner kept his back turned to her, his eyes fixed on the timbered slopes plunging away beneath him.

'What is it you *want?*' she said again.

At last he turned. As soon as they'd reached Eagle's Nest he'd forced her to dismount and then followed her down off his horse. He'd shoved her to the ground and then fumbled in one saddle bag until he found what he was searching for. The wind was strong on this exposed plateau, and somehow colder than it had been, and there was a promise of snow in the leaden sky.

Rachel looked around, wondered if she dare make a break for it while he was otherwise occupied, and how far she'd get if she did. There was nowhere she might run to. All she was likely to do was make him even more dangerous than he already seemed to be. But she was damned if she'd let him use her as bait!

What did he want with Val, anyway? Who *was* he?

If flight was out of the question, that left only one option — fight. She looked around, searching for something she might use as a weapon, a rock, a stout deadfall branch —

But he was already turning back to her, piggin strings hanging in his black-gloved hands like dead snakes, and his eyes, when he looked at her, were flat and hard, like chips of wet coal.

Handling her roughly, he'd tied her hand and foot, slapping her once when she tried to resist him. Then he'd looked around, and finding a suitable spot, had dragged her across to it. It was a narrow outcrop of rock that overlooked a more or less sheer drop. He'd left her there, knowing she could struggle all she liked, but she'd never loosen the knots he'd tied. And even if she did, the outcrop was so narrow that the chances were good that, in all the squirming she'd have to do in her attempt to escape, she'd likely slip and fall to her death long before they unraveled.

Now she glared at him, her raven hair hanging loose around her face, her features smudged and bruised. But still there was no fear in her — leastways, none that she would allow him to see. All she conveyed was anger.

'Who are you?' she asked.

Nothing.

'What is it you want from us?'

'Your son,' he said.

'I know that. What I don't know is why? What has Val ever done to you?'

'Nothin' to me *personally*,' said Tanner.

'Then why . . . all this?'

He turned away from her, wandered a few paces, then fished out the photograph of Ned and looked at it.

His own reflection, showing mistily in the glass, melted into Ned's image, so that the two faces became almost as one. He liked that, and smiled.

He wasn't even aware that he'd drifted off into thought until something, some sense in him that had kept him alive all these years but had somehow fallen dormant until now, brought him up sharp. He shoved the picture away, fished his telescope from a jacket pocket, put it to one eye and surveyed the slopes below.

About three, four hundred yards below him, a rider had halted his horse and was sitting his saddle with shoulders hunched and head bowed. Tanner's dark hazel eyes suddenly sharpened. But the shape of the man . . . Val McCall wasn't that heavyset.

Then the rider straightened up, and Tanner saw the shock-white beard, and his grin widened. 'Looks like your old man's comin' to your rescue,' he called over one shoulder. 'Now ain't that touchin'?'

He turned away from the rim, shoved the telescope back into his pocket and then drew his Winchester '92 from its saddle scabbard.

'Well,' he said conversationally. 'Let's make sure we give him a warm welcome when he gets here, shall we?'

And he levered a shell into the breech.

* * *

The climb seemed to take forever. Trails that Val thought he remembered from the past continually petered out without warning, and he had to turn tail and try to find another way up to Eagle's Nest. Despite the chill wind he was soon sweating and the horse was lathered. And yet when he drew rein to give them both a breather, his destination looked just as far away as when he'd first started his ascent.

He sagged, wondering if he really stood a hope in hell of actually finding the elusive trail, or whether he was just wasting time he could ill afford to lose. There *was* a way up to the peak from this northern-facing slope, dammit — he knew there was! And as if to confirm it, the trail he was on now, as narrow and indistinct as it was, was littered with tracks — of black bear and marmot, mule deer and coyote.

All he had to do was keep at it.

He leaned forward, stroked his horse's sweated neck and said, 'Come on, feller. Let's keep movin'.'

★ ★ ★

'*Cyrus!*'

CYRUS . . . Cyrus . . . cyrus . . .

Cyrus McCall's head snapped up just in time to catch a flash of color on the edge of an outcrop about thirty yards above him. He recognized it immediately — Rachel's brown tapestry coat — the coat she'd been wearing when she'd left for town that morning!

He drew a breath into his aching lungs and bellowed, '*Rachel? That you?*

I'm comin', honey!'

He tried to make his voice sound strong. Whether or not he succeeded, he couldn't say. In truth he felt just about as weak as a kitten, and hated himself for it. All his life he'd been tough and capable, but now that he needed all his strength it had deserted him. But what else could he do? His wife needed him, his boy needed him, and if he had to give his life for them, so be it.

He slid down out of the saddle and when his feet hit the ground it was all he could do not to collapse. He leaned against the horse for a moment, sweating hard, breathing harder, but maybe that was to his advantage. Maybe the sonofabitch who'd kidnapped Rachel would see that and dismiss him as a weak sister, not worth worrying over. He only needed one chance, anyway, and then the gun he'd stuffed into the waistband of his pants would do all the talking for him.

He started up the incline, slow and

cumbersome in his movements. Pulses hammered in his ears. He grabbed for brush and rocks and pulled more than climbed up toward Eagle's Nest, and he knew he must look pathetic and right then didn't give a damn about it.

Then a volley of shots rang out, one, two, three, four, and Cyrus fell forward onto his belly, hat flying from his head, unable to stop a cry as his landing sent the pain of his healing wounds lancing through him. Bullets chopped through brush, drilled into the dirt around him and whined off rocks. He kept his head down, waiting for that white-hot punch of lead he remembered so well from last time.

But nothing happened, and as the shots echoed away he realized that the marksman was only playing with him.

Sure enough:

'Stop right there, old man, or we'll see whether or not this woman of yours can fly!'

Cyrus craned his neck, saw a tall, unshaven man in a black frock coat and matching hat standing over Rachel with a rifle held across his chest.

'*Cut her loose!*' he bawled, pushing up onto his knees, wondering if he could reach the gun at his back and use it — effectively — before the man up there could make good on his threat.

LOOSE . . . Loose . . . loose . . . said his echo.

He staggered to his feet, swaying without his cane. 'Settle your gripe like a man, damn you! I'm all stove up, but I'll still — '

Almost faster than thought, Tanner brought the rifle around and down again and fired another shot.

Rachel screamed.

14

Val, on the far side of the peak, was less than fifty feet from Eagle's Nest when he heard his mother yell: '*Cyrus!*'

Next came a volley of rifle fire; deep, booming blasts that came one after another, and instinctively he reached for his Colt.

A few moments later there was only silence.

Val strained his eyes and ears. That his father had decided to make the climb to Eagle's Peak was obvious. That he'd been seen and — God, he could hardly bear the thought — maybe killed by whoever had kidnapped his mother was almost enough to make him throw caution aside and send him charging up what remained of the grade to settle the score.

But that wouldn't help anyone. So he stayed where he was, sweating hard from the climb he'd had to make on foot when the trail they were on grew too steep and narrow to accommodate his horse.

Then:

'*Stop right there, old man, or we'll see whether or not this woman of yours can fly!*'

Val sagged a little. His father was still alive, then. There was still a chance.

Galvanized now, he continued searching for hand- and footholds, dragging himself ever closer to the jagged ridge that met the overcast sky beyond.

And he was so intent on the task that he had no idea he was being followed every foot of the way.

★　★　★

'Stay put, old man!' called Abraham Tanner, coming down the slope to meet him. 'My business ain't with you!'

'No,' Cyrus replied, glaring up at him. 'It's with my son, isn't it? Because Maggie Carter hired you to *kill* him!'

258

'Way I hear it,' said Tanner, 'he didn't give Maggie's boy a chance.'

'And you heard that from Maggie herself, I'm bettin'.'

'You know somethin', McCall?' replied Tanner, stopping ten feet away. 'I ain't never been what you might call a charitable man. But just this once I'm gonna be right charitable to you. You come on up here, now. Come on, it's okay. You come on up here an' join your wife. I want you to be together, when your boy gets here. That way I can spare you the grief that Maggie's got to live with.'

McCall frowned. 'What?'

'Well, you think about it,' said Tanner, and all at once his unpredictable, whiskey-fuelled fury began to rise. 'She's got to live with the knowledge that her boy ain't never comin' home again. Won't ever celebrate another birthday, won't ever get married, give her grandkids, won't ever take over that there ranch she and her old man built up. She's got to live with that. And when I kill your boy, so will you — but only for as long as it takes for me to kill *you*, too.'

Above and behind him, Rachel sobbed. Before him, McCall's face went slack — and then he reached for the gun at his back.

He never stood a chance.

Moving like a panther, Tanner crowded him, slammed him in the side of the head with the butt of the rifle and Cyrus went down, hearing Rachel scream again.

Tanner grabbed him by the collar, dragged him the rest of the way up the slope and dumped him beside her. She stared at her unconscious husband, the side of his face already discoloring and starting to swell.

'You *bastard!*' she breathed.

Tanner gave an exaggerated wince. 'Such language,' he said. 'And here's me, all this time thinkin' you was a lady.'

Two things happened then.

One — he thought he heard a soft scrape of displaced rock somewhere behind him.

Two — Rachel's dark eyes flickered

to a spot beyond him, then quickly back to his face.

Heeding his instincts, he turned, dropped to his knees, spotted a figure coming over the ridge behind him and fired, fast. The rifle spat flame, and the figure on the ridge — he saw now that it was, as he'd suspected, Val McCall — twisted, dropped the Colt he'd been holding, then followed it as it skittered down the slope with right hand clapped to bleeding left shoulder.

'Well, well,' Tanner said, rising, striding to the fallen youngster, kicking Val's gun well beyond reach. 'If it isn't the guest of honor. The man who killed Ned Carter.'

Val looked up at him, brown eyes glazed by the pain of his shoulder wound, dizzy from the blood he'd already lost, and hating himself because he'd had one good chance to turn the tables on this man and it hadn't worked.

He said nothing. He didn't believe there was anything to say. He'd already heard enough to know that there was no mercy in this man. No mercy — and so nothing to lose by at least trying to go down fighting.

'Cat got your tongue?' asked Tanner. 'Don't you even want to try an' deny it? Or beg for a little clemency?'

Without warning, Val rammed his foot hard into Tanner's shin with enough force to break bone. Tanner's heavy boot absorbed most of it, but still the impact, coming hard and unexpected as it did, sent him stumbling back with a howl of pain.

Ignoring the pain in his shoulder as best he could, Val rolled, came up and threw himself at the man even as Tanner tried to recover and fire the rifle. He tackled Tanner around the waist and momentum shoved them backwards until Tanner lost balance and slammed down with Val on top.

The two men struggled, each trying to claw the other's eyes out. Blood from Val's shoulder-wound dripped into Tanner's face and he screwed his face up and shook his head to clear it from his eyes. Val punched him, hurt his own hand more than he likely hurt Tanner, and then Tanner gave an eel-like wriggle and Val slammed over onto his back.

Tanner came up, went after him, tried to stomp him, missed when Val rolled again. He lunged back in, this time booted Val in the ribs, and as Val hunched up Tanner bent, yanked him to his feet, spun him around and punched him full in the face. Val went backwards, almost unconscious, and was hardly aware of it when the ground dropped out from under him and he went rolling down the slope toward his father's waiting horse.

With a roar Tanner went chasing down the slope after him, leaving Rachel to dig frantically at her husband in an attempt to wake him. There wasn't much she could do, bound as she was. But if Cyrus could just get the rifle, they could still turn this thing around —

But McCall was out of it.

Rachel felt despair wash over her.

Until, from the ridge Val had just
appeared from —

★ ★ ★

Val came up onto his feet, not really
knowing where he was. Tanner crashed
into him and they both slammed up
against the horse. With a shrill whinny
the horse bolted as Tanner grabbed him
by the shoulder and, teeth clenched,
hissed, 'Come on, boy, let's get this
thing done! By the time they find your
cold, dead bodies, I aim to be long gone
from here!'

A scream ripped the chilly air, then
— not a scream, more of a war cry.

Tanner turned just as Kate came
charging down the slope toward him
with his rifle held like a club in both
small hands. He had one fraction of
time in which to take in her face,
smeared and flushed by the climb she'd
just made, to wince at the mad scream
that wrenched her face out of shape,
and then —

264

— then she swung the rifle in a wide circle and hit him with it, full-force.

Tanner howled, let go of Val, crumpled sideways with the force of the blow. If it had hit him in the head it would have killed him outright. Unfortunately he took the blow on the right shoulder, and though that hurt like hell, all it really served to do was anger him still more.

Kate watched, wide-eyed, as he turned and straightened back to his full height, sweaty face slick with blood, one lip busted and swelling from the fight. Sounding as if he really wanted to know, he rasped, 'Who the *hell're* you?'

Kate froze. She wanted to tell him she was Kate Carter and that he could now consider whatever arrangement he'd made with her mother as cancelled. Instead her throat was so constricted she could say nothing.

Tanner said, 'No matter.'

Then the spell broke and she quickly tried to bring the rifle around so that she could shoot him with it.

265

He was too quick for her. His left arm shot out, he ripped the weapon from her and flung it aside, then slapped her savagely.

His open palm connected with a sound like a gunshot, and Kate's head cracked sideways. She stumbled, but Tanner went after her, dug fingers tight into her shoulder, held her steady, brought his right hand back in a fist.

There *was* a gunshot then, and even as it tore across the high country Abraham Tanner was thrown sideways, his head exploding into a crimson mist.

A moment passed . . . two . . .

Swaying, Kate looked down at the corpse, the chilly wind ruffling what was left of its long black hair. For a moment her vision swam, but she wasn't the fainting type: that wasn't going to do anyone any good right then. Besides, who had fired the shot that had saved them?

Pale now, she looked around. Rachel was still bound hand and foot. Cyrus was only now beginning to stir sluggishly. She felt Val looking up at her, felt a sudden need to care for him that was almost akin to an ache. But even as she started toward him, she saw a rider far, far below them, heading down out of the foothills, a rifle across its lap.

She froze, believing she knew who that figure was.

Then she turned, snatched up the telescope that had fallen from Tanner's pocket when he fell, and put it to her eye.

She was right.

It was her mother, huddled in her creased old box jacket and full-cut riding skirt, her unflattering hat with its center dent pulled low over her red-auburn hair. And the long gun across her lap was Nubbs' old Whitworth rifle, with the William Malcolm rifle scope that was almost as long as the gun itself attached.

Val struggled to his feet, breathing hard. He said, 'Kate . . . '

* * *

But Kate was still watching her mother as she allowed Blaze to pick his way down off the mountain, and in particular she was watching the quick, noticeable rise and fall of her mother's shoulders.

She's crying, she thought. *For the first time in twenty-five years, she's crying.*

15

What had decided Maggie in the end was Abraham Tanner himself.

At first she'd been blinded by grief. She'd convinced herself that the only way she and Ned would ever know peace was by having Val McCall killed. Let the McCalls deal with the loss of a son as she'd had to deal with it.

But when it seemed that Tanner had done as she'd ordered, there had been no sense of triumph in her, only regret.

And so she had saddled Blaze and rode out to Eagle's Nest, as much to protect her daughter as to save Cyrus and Rachel McCall from having to suffer as she had suffered. She had gone with the intention of doing as Kate had said, to call Tanner off. And as she climbed ever closer to Eagle's Nest she had seen Rachel, tied and distraught; seen Cyrus, old, weak, still game even though he knew he never stood a chance against a man of Tanner's caliber. She'd seen Val McCall risk everything for his parents . . . and then she'd seen Kate risk everything for the McCalls.

Kate — the girl she might have been, had life been a little kinder to her.

And when Abraham Tanner raised his hand to Kate, all the memories of her own abusive adolescence had come crashing back to her, and in that moment she knew what she had to do, what she should have done all the years before.

Now it was done. Abraham Tanner was dead.

And so was her past.

* * *

No one ever saw Maggie Carter again after that day. No one knew where she went to or what became of her. It was as if she just . . . ceased to be.

But about two months later, Kate

received a letter from a lawyer in California, informing her that her mother had deeded the C.A. Carter Ranch to her, in the hope that she would run it well and with more compassion that she herself had ever shown. Kate contacted the lawyer, but he refused to release details of Maggie's present whereabouts.

So Kate found herself with sole responsibility for the ranch, and decided that it was not such a bad thing after all. As the new owner, she was in the best possible position to repair at least some of the damage her mother's actions had caused. She was almost tempted to use the phrase *mending fences*, but that was too reminiscent of the barbed wire that had caused so much bad blood in the first place, and was now just an unpleasant memory in those hills and meadows of Montana.

For their part, the McCalls bore her no ill will. Whatever Maggie Carter had done was Maggie Carter's responsibility, and neither Cyrus nor Rachel had any intention of taking it out on Kate. Indeed, Rachel secretly enjoyed having Kate around, and as the months progressed, she became more of a mother to the girl than she suspected Maggie had ever allowed herself to be.

In any case, as Cyrus often pointed out, if it hadn't been for Kate, things might have turned out a whole lot different that wintry day up on Eagle's Nest. And the more he saw of the girl, the more he found to like. She had all the strength and determination of her mother, but none of the bitterness. One day he reckoned she'd make someone a fine wife.

That thought would inevitably turn his thoughts toward Val. Damn, but that boy would forgive Kate Carter just about anything! And there was no quit in him. Just as he continued to chase that paint mustang with the cream-colored mane whenever their paths crossed, he pursued Kate with the same persistence. She never encouraged him, of course — she didn't need to. But neither did she *discourage* him, exactly. Cyrus guessed she wanted him to *earn* her affection — and Val was happy to do that.

Still, it was hard for Kate to accept that she would never see her mother again, and often, on sleepless nights, she found herself wondering where Maggie was now, what she was doing, and whether or not she had finally found peace. She liked to think so.

When she and Val finally married little over a year later, and the C.A. Carter joined with Big Sky to become the biggest ranch in the county, Simon Doubleday was there to cover the event for the *Enterprise*. Later, Kate sent a copy of that edition to the lawyer in California with a request that he forward it on to her mother. She had no idea whether or not he would. She could only hope.

But a month later a note arrived at Big Sky, written in her mother's painstakingly neat hand. It read:

Dearest Kathryn,

You have picked well in your choice of husband. If he is even half the man your father was, you will enjoy a happy life, and I believe he is far more than that.

For me, the past is finally laid to rest. For you, the future has already begun. I wish for it to be as bright as possible, and want you to know that you have made me very proud — prouder than I have any right to be.

Love
Mother

Approval at last.

It was the finest gift Kate could have received.

THE END

Seth Klugg, manager of the Springfield Cattlemen's Bank, is out of town, seeing the proposed new railroad as an opportunity for drumming up business. Meanwhile, the three strangers who ride into Springfield see in his absence an opportunity of their own . . . Kidnapping the assistant bank manager and his wife, they proceed to hold them hostage, awaiting the return of Klugg — the only man who knows the combination for the bank's safe. But Klugg has made many enemies, and is riding alone across open terrain — what will happen if he fails to return?

A STORM IN MONTANA

Will DuRey

Clancy Jarrett possesses a quick and violent temper, and no citizen of Brannigan dares cross him. When his stagecoach hold-up is thwarted by three trail-herders, his rage cannot be contained. And when he learns that they are escorting Kate Jeavons — a dance-hall girl whose sister Alice he has captive — to testify against him, they are firmly in his sights. Black clouds are forming overhead, but which storm will break first: the wild prairie rain, or the deadly guns of Jarrett and his crew?

THE SCARS OF IRON EYES

Rory Black

Hot on the trail of outlaw Two Fingers McGraw, bounty hunter Iron Eyes realizes that he is headed into the forest where he grew to manhood. Most of the woodland has been felled, there is a war going on between two rival outfits for the remainder — and now their guns are turned on him! Stuck in the middle of a deadly battle, Iron Eyes seeks refuge in the trees from the enemies who are eager to add to his scars . . .

BACKSHOOTER

Dale Graham

Reece Willard and Dandy Sam Foley were partners running the Rolling Dice Saloon in Three Forks, Montana. When they took out an extra loan for an adjoining dance hall, neither had any idea that the crooked bank manager would trick them. Threatened with eviction, the partners were forced to take the law into their own hands. But Reece served time in the state penitentiary for it, whilst the treacherous Sam escaped justice. Now released from prison, Reece is hot on Sam's trail — will he get his revenge?

LATIMER'S JUSTICE

Terrell L. Bowers

Dean Latimer has a reputation for being handy with both his fists and guns — and staying cool under fire. So when Marshal Konrad Ellington needs him to help Constance Dewitt prove her brother Sheldon innocent of a murder charge, he is the perfect man for the job. But the town of Baxterville is run by crooked men, with gunslingers backing their play; and when Latimer tries to save the innocent Sheldon, he ends up accused of murder and running for his life . . .